MILLY DARRELL

MILLY DARRELL

M. E. BRADDON

Serenity
Publishers, LLC
ROCKVILLE, MARYLAND
2009

ISBN: 978-1-60450-580-1

Published by Serenity Publishers
An Arc Manor Company
P. O. Box 10339
Rockville, MD 20849-0339
www.SerenityPublishers.com

Printed in the United States of America/United Kingdom

TO

DR. AND MRS. BEAMAN,

The Author's Old and Valued Friends,
This book is Affectionately Inscribed.

MILLY DARRELL

CHAPTER I

I Begin Life

I was just nineteen years of age when I began my career as articled pupil with the Miss Bagshots of Albury Lodge, Fendale, Yorkshire. My father was a country curate, with a delicate wife and four children, of whom I was the eldest; and I had known from my childhood that the day must come in which I should have to get my own living in almost the only vocation open to a poor gentleman's daughter. I had been fairly educated near home, and the first opportunity that arose for placing me out in the world had been gladly seized upon by my poor father, who consented to pay the modest premium required by the Miss Bagshots, in order that I might be taught the duties of a governess, and essay my powers of tuition upon the younger pupils at Albury Lodge.

How well I remember the evening of my arrival!—a bleak dreary evening at the close of January, made still more dismal by a drizzling rain that had never ceased falling since I left my father's snug little house at Briarwood in Warwickshire. I had had to change trains three times, and to wait during a blank and miserable hour and a quarter, or so, at small obscure stations, staring hopelessly at the advertisements on the walls— advertisements of somebody's life-sustaining cocoa, and somebody else's health-restoring cod-liver oil, or trying to read the big brown-backed Bible in the cheerless little waiting-room; and trying, O so hard, not to think of home, and all the love and happiness I had left behind me. The journey had been altogether tiresome and fatiguing; but, for all that, the knowledge that I was near my destination brought me no sense of pleasure. I think I should have wished that dismal journey prolonged indefinitely, if I could thereby have escaped the beginning of my new life.

A lumbering omnibus conveyed me from the station to Albury Lodge, after depositing a grim-looking elderly lady at a house on the outskirts of the town, and a dapper-looking little man, whom I took for a commercial traveller, at an inn in the market-place. I watched the road with a kind of idle curiosity as the vehicle lumbered along. The town had a cheerful prosperous air even on this wet winter night, and I saw that there were two fine old churches, and a large modern building which I supposed to be the town-hall.

We left the town quite behind us before we came to Albury Lodge; a very large house on the high-road, a square red-brick house of the early Georgian era, shut in from the road by high walls. The great wrought-iron gates in the front had been boarded up, and Albury Lodge was now approached by a little wooden side-door into a stone-flagged covered passage that led to a small door at the end of the house. The omnibus-driver deposited me at this door, with all my worldly possessions, which at this period of my life consisted of two rather small boxes and a japanned dressing-case, a receptacle that contained all my most sacred treasures.

I was admitted by a rather ill-tempered-looking house-maid, with a cap of obtrusive respectability and a spotless white apron. I fancied that she looked just a little superciliously at my boxes, which I daresay would not have contained her own wardrobe.

'O, it's the governess-pupil, I suppose?' she said. 'You was expected early this afternoon, miss. Miss Bagshot and Miss Susan are gone out to tea; but I can show you where you are to sleep, if you'll please to step this way. Do you think you could carry one of your trunks, if I carry the other?'

I thought I could; so the housemaid and I lugged them all the way along the stone passage and up an uncarpeted back staircase which led from the lobby into which the door at the end of the passage opened. We went very high up, to the top story in fact, where the housemaid led me into a long bare room with ten little beds in it. I was well enough accustomed to the dreariness of a school dormitory, but somehow this room looked unusually dismal.

There was a jet of gas burning at one end of the room, near a door opening into a lavatory which was little more than a cupboard, but in which ten young ladies had to perform their daily ablutions. Here I washed my face and hands in icy-cold water, and arranged my hair as well as I could without the aid of a looking-glass, that being a luxury not provided at Albury Lodge. The servant stood watching me as I made this brief toilet, waiting to conduct me to the schoolroom. I followed her, shivering as I went, to a great empty room on the first floor. The holidays were not quite over, and none of the pupils had as yet returned. There was an almost painful neatness and bareness in place of the usual litter of books and papers, and I could not help thinking that an apartment in a workhouse would have looked quite as cheerful. Even the fire behind the high wire guard seemed to burn in a different manner from all home fires: a fact which I attributed then to some sympathetic property in the coal, but which I afterwards found to be caused by a plentiful admixture of coke; a slow sulky smoke went up from the dull mass of fuel, brightened ever so little now and then by a sickly yellow flame. One jet of gas dimly lighted this long dreary room, in which there was no human creature but myself and my guide.

'I'll bring you some supper presently, miss,' the housemaid said, and departed before I could put in a timid plea for that feminine luxury, a cup of tea.

I had not expected to find myself quite alone on this first night of my arrival, and a feeling of hopeless wretchedness came over me as I sat down at one end of a long green-baize-covered table, and rested my head upon my folded arms. Of course it was very weak and foolish, a bad beginning of my new life, but I was quite powerless to contend against that sense of utter misery. I thought of all I had left at home. I thought of what my life might have been if my father had been only a little better off: and then I burst out crying as if my heart were breaking.

Suddenly, in the midst of that foolish paroxysm, I felt a light hand upon my shoulder, and looking up, saw a face bending over me, a face full of sympathy and compassion.

O Milly Darrell, my darling, my love, how am I to describe you as you appeared before my eyes that night? How poorly can any words of mine paint you in your girlish beauty, as you looked down upon me in that dimly-lighted schoolroom with divine compassion in your dark eloquent eyes!

Just at that moment I was so miserable and so inclined to be sulky in my wretchedness, that even the vision of that bright face gave me little pleasure. I pushed away the gentle hand ungraciously, and rose hastily from my seat.

'Pray don't cry any more,' said the young lady; 'I can't bear to hear you cry like that.'

'I'm not going to cry any more,' I answered, drying my eyes in a hasty, angry way. 'It was very foolish of me to cry at all; but this place did look so cheerless and dreary, and I began to think of my father and mother, and all I had left behind me at home.'

'Of course it was only natural you should think of them. Everything does seem so bleak and dismal the first night; but you are very happy to have so many at home. I have only papa.'

'Indeed!' I said, not feeling deeply interested in her affairs.

I looked at her as she stood leaning a little against the end of the table, and playing idly with a bunch of charms and lockets hanging to her gold chain. She was very handsome, a brunette, with a small straight nose, hazel eyes, and dark-brown hair. Her mouth was the prettiest and most expressive I ever saw in my life, and gave an indescribable charm to her face. She was handsomely dressed in violet silk, with rich white lace about the throat and sleeves.

'You will find things much pleasanter when the girls come back. Of course school is always a little dreary compared with home; one is prepared for that; but I have no doubt you will contrive to be happy, and I hope we shall be very good friends. I think you must be the Miss Crofton I have heard spoken of lately?'

'Yes, my name is Crofton—Mary Crofton.'

'And mine is Emily Darrell. Milly I am always called at home, and by any one who likes me. I am a parlour-boarder, and have the run of the house, as it were. I am rather old to be at school, you see; but I am going home at the end of this year. I was brought up at home with a governess until about six months ago; but then papa took it into his head that I should be happier amongst girls of my own age, and sent me off to school. He has been travelling since that time, and so I have not been home for the Christmas holidays. I can't tell you what a disappointment that was.'

I tried to look sympathetic, and, not knowing exactly what to say, I asked whether Miss Darrell's father lived in that neighbourhood.

'O dear, no,' she answered; 'he lives nearly a hundred miles away, in a very wild part of Yorkshire, not far from the sea. But Thornleigh—that is the name for our house—is a dear old place, and I like our bleak wild country better than the loveliest spot in the world. I was born there, you see, and all my happy memories of my childhood and my mother are associated with that dear old home.'

'Is it long since you lost your mother?'

'Ten years. I loved her so dearly. There are some subjects about which one dare not speak. I cannot often trust myself to talk of her.'

I liked her better after this. At first her beauty and her handsome dress had seemed a little overpowering to me; I had felt as if she were a being of another order, a bright happy creature not subject to the common woes of life. But now that she had spoken of her own sorrows, I felt that we were upon a level; and I stole my hand timidly into hers, and murmured some apology for my previous rudeness.

'You were not rude, dear. I know I must have seemed very intrusive when I disturbed you; but I could not bear to hear you crying like that. And now tell me where you sleep.'

I described the room as well as I could.

'I know where you mean,' she said; 'it's close to my room. I have the privilege of a little room to myself, you know; and on half-holidays I have a fire there, and write my letters, or paint; and you must come and sit with me on these afternoons, and we can be as happy as possible together working and talking. Do you paint?'

'A little—in a schoolgirlish fashion kind of way.'

'Quite as well as I do, I daresay,' Miss Darrell answered, laughing gaily, 'only you are more modest about it. O, here comes your supper; may I sit with you while you eat it?'

'I shall be very glad if you will.'

'I hope you have brought Miss Crofton a good supper, Sarah,' she went on in the same gay girlish way.—'Sarah is a very good creature, you must know, Miss Crofton, though she seems a little grim to strangers. That's only a way of hers: she *can* smile, I assure you, though you'd hardly think so.'

Sarah's hard-looking mouth expanded into a kind of grin at this.

'There's no getting over you, Miss Darrell,' she said; 'you've got such a way of your own. I've brought Miss Crofton some cold beef; but if she'd like a bit of pickle, I wouldn't mind going to ask cook for it. Cold meat does eat a little dry without pickle.'

This 'bit of pickle' was evidently a concession in my favour made to please Emily Darrell. I thanked Sarah, and told her that I would not trouble her with a journey to the cook. I was faint and worn-out with my day's pilgrimage, and had eaten very little since morning; but the most epicurean repast ever prepared by a French chef would have seemed so much dust and ashes to me that night; so I sat down meekly to my supper of bread and meat, and listened to Milly Darrell's chatter as I ate it.

Of course she told me all about the school, Miss Bagshot, and Miss Susan Bagshot. The elder of these two ladies was her favourite. Miss Susan had, in the remote period of her youth, been the victim of some unhappy love-affair, which had soured her disposition, and inclined her to look on the joys and follies of girlhood with a jaundiced eye. It was easy enough to please Miss Bagshot, who had a genial matronly way, and took real delight in her pupils; but it was almost impossible to satisfy Miss Susan.

'And I am sorry to say that you will be a good deal with her,' Miss Darrell said, shaking her head gravely; 'for you are to take the second English class under her—I heard them say so at dinner to-day— and I am afraid she will fidget you almost out of your life; but you must try to keep your temper, and take things as quietly as you can, and I daresay in time you will be able to get on with her.'

'I'm sure I hope so,' I answered rather sadly; and then Miss Darrell asked me how long I was to be at Albury Lodge.

'Three years,' I told her; 'and after that, Miss Bagshot is to place me somewhere as a governess.'

'You are going to be a governess always?'

'I suppose so,' I answered. The word 'always' struck me with a little sharp pain, almost like a wound. Yes, I supposed it would be always. I was neither pretty nor attractive. What issue could there be for me out of that dull hackneyed round of daily duties which makes up the sum of a governess's life?

'I am obliged to do something for my living,' I said; 'my father is very poor. I hope I may be able to help him a little by and by.'

'And my father is so ridiculously rich. He is a great ironmaster, and has wharves and warehouses, and goodness knows what, at North Shields. How hard it seems!'

'What seems hard?' I asked absently.

'That money should be so unequally divided. Do you know, I don't think I should much mind going out as a governess: it would be a way of seeing life. One must meet with all sorts of adventures, going among strangers like that.'

I looked at her as she smiled at me, with a smile that gave an indescribable brightness to her face, and I fancied that for her indeed there could be no form of life so dull that would not hold some triumph, some success. She seemed a creature born to extract brightness out of the commonest things, a creature to be only admired and caressed, go where she might.

'You a governess!' I said, a little scornfully; 'you are not of the clay that makes governesses.'

'Why not?'

'You are much too pretty and too fascinating.'

'O, Mary Crofton, Mary Crofton—may I call you Mary, please? we are going to be such friends—if you begin by flattering me like that, how am I ever to trust you and lean upon you? I want some one with a stronger mind than my own, you know, dear, to lead me right; for I'm the weakest, vainest creature in the world, I believe. Papa has spoiled me so.'

'If you are always like what you are to-night, I don't think the spoiling has done much mischief,' I said.

'O, I am always amiable enough, so long as I have my own way. And now tell me all about your home.'

I gave her a faithful account of my brothers and my sister, and a brief description of the dear old-fashioned cottage, with its white-plaster walls crossed with great black beams, its many gables and quaint latticed windows. I told her how happy and united we had always been at home, and how this made my separation from those I loved so much the harder to bear; to all of which Milly Darrell listened with most unaffected sympathy.

Early the next day my new life began in real earnest. Miss Susan Bagshot did not allow me to waste my time in idleness until the arrival of my pupils. She gave me a pile of exercises to correct, and some difficult needlework to finish; and I found I had indeed a sharp task-mistress in this blighted lady.

'Girls of your age are so incorrigibly idle,' she said; 'but I must give you to understand at once that you will have no time for dawdling at Albury Lodge. The first bell rings a quarter before six, and at a quarter past I shall expect to see you in the schoolroom. You will superintend the younger pupils' pianoforte practice from that time till eight o'clock, at which hour we breakfast. From nine till twelve you will take the second division of the second class for English, according to the routine arranged by me, which you had better copy from a paper I will lend you for that purpose. After dinner you will take the same class for two hours' reading until four; from four to five you will superintend the needlework class. Your evenings—with the exception of the careful correction of all the day's exercises—will be your own. I hope you have a sincere love of your vocation, Miss Crofton.'

I said I hoped I should grow to like my work as I became accustomed to it. I had never yet tried teaching, except with my young sister and brothers. My hear sank as I remembered our free-and-easy studies in the sunny parlour at home, or out in the garden under the pink and white hawthorns sometimes on balmy mornings in the early summer.

Miss Susan shook her head doubtfully.

'Unless you have a love of your vocation you will never succeed, Miss Crofton,' she said solemnly.

I freely confess that this love she spoke of never came to me. I tried to do my duty, and I endured all the hardships of my life in, I hope, a cheerful spirit. But the dry monotony of the studies had no element of pleasantness, and I used to wonder how Miss Susan could derive pleasure—as it was evident she did—from the exercise of her authority over those hapless scholars who had the misfortune to belong to her class. Day after day they heard the same lectures, listened submissively to the same reproofs, and toiled on upon that bleak bare high-road to learning, along which it was her delight to drive them. Nothing like a flower brightened their weary way—it was all alike dust and barrenness; but they ploughed on dutifully, cramming their youthful minds with the hardest dates and facts to be found in the history of mankind, the dreariest statistics, the driest details of geography, and the most recondite rules of grammar, until the happy hour arrived in which they took their final departure from Albury Lodge, to forget all they had learnt there in the briefest possible time.

How my thoughts used to wander away sometimes as I sat at my desk, distracted by the unmelodious sound of Miss Susan's voice lecturing some victim in her own division at the next table, while one of the girls in mine droned drearily at Lingard, or Pinnock's *Goldsmith,* as the case might be! How the vision of my own bright home haunted me during those long monotonous afternoons, while the March winds made the poplars rock in the garden outside the schoolroom, or the April rain beat against the great bare windows!

CHAPTER II

Milly's Visitor

It was not often that I had a half-holiday to myself, for Miss Susan Bagshot seemed to take a delight in finding me something to do on these occasions; but whenever I had, I spent it with Milly Darrell, and on these rare afternoons I was perfectly happy. I had grown to love her as I did not think it was in me to love any one who was not of my own flesh and blood; and in so loving her, I only returned the affection which she felt for me.

I am sure it was the fact of my friendlessness, and of my subordinate position in the school, which had drawn this girl's generous heart towards me; and I should have been hard indeed if I had not felt touched by her regard. She soon grew indescribably dear to me. She was of my own age, able to sympathize with every thought and fancy of mine; the frankest, most open-hearted of creatures; a little proud of her beauty, perhaps, when it was praised by those she loved, but never proud of her wealth, or insolent to those whose gifts were less than hers.

I used to write my home-letters in her room on these rare and happy afternoons, while she painted at an easel near the window. The room was small, but better furnished than the ordinary rooms in the house, and it was brightened by all sorts of pretty things,— handsomely-bound books upon hanging shelves, pictures, Dresden cups and saucers, toilet-bottles and boxes, which Miss Darrell had brought from home. Over the mantelpiece there was a large photograph of her father, and by the bedside there hung a more flattering water-coloured portrait, painted by Milly herself. It was a powerful and rather a handsome face, but I thought the expression a little hard and cold, even in Milly's portrait.

She painted well, and had a real love of art. Her studies at Albury Lodge were of rather a desultory kind, as she was not supposed to belong to any class; but she had lessons from nearly half-a-dozen different masters—German lessons, Italian lessons, drawing lessons, music and singing lessons—and was altogether a very profitable pupil. She had her own way with every one, I found, and I believe Miss Bagshot was really fond of her.

Her father was travelling in Italy at this time, and did not often write to her—a fact that distressed her very much, I know; but she used to shake off her sorrow in a bright hopeful way that was peculiar to her, always making excuses for the dilatory correspondent. She loved him intensely, and keenly felt this separation from him; but the doctors had recommended him rest and change of air and scene, she told me, and she was glad to think he was obeying them.

Upon one of these half-holidays, when midsummer was near at hand, we were interrupted by an unwonted event, in the shape of a visit from a cousin of Milly's; a young man who occupied an important position in her

father's house of business, and of whom she had sometimes talked to me, but not much. His name was Julian
Stormont, and he was the only son of Mr. Darrell's only
sister, long since dead.

It was a sultry afternoon, and we were spending it in a
rustic summer-house at the end of a broad gravel that
went the whole length of the large garden. Milly had
her drawing materials on the table before her, but had
not been using them. I was busy with a piece of fancy-
work which Miss Susan Bagshot had given me to finish.
We were sitting like this, when my old acquaintance
Sarah, the housemaid, came to announce a visitor for
Miss Darrell.

Milly sprang to her feet, flushed with excitement.

'It must be papa!' she cried joyfully.

'Lor', no, miss; don't you go to excite yourself like that.
It isn't your pa; it's a younger gentleman.'

She handed Milly a card.

'Mr. Stormont!' the girl exclaimed, with a disappointed
air; 'my cousin Julian. I am coming to him, of course,
Sarah. But I wish you had given me the card at once.'

'Won't you go and do somethink to your hair, miss?
most young ladies do.'

'O yes, I know; there are girls who would stop to have
their hair done in Grecian plaits, if the dearest friend
they had in the world was waiting for them in the drawing-room. My hair will do well enough, Sarah.—Come,
Mary, you'll come to the house with me, won't you?'

'Lor', miss, here comes the gentleman,' said Sarah; and
then decamped by an obscure side-path.

'I had better leave you to see him alone, Milly,' I said; but she told me imperatively to stay, and I stayed.

She went a little way to meet the gentleman, who seemed pleased to see her, but whom she received rather coldly, as I thought. But I had not long to think about it, before she had brought him to the summer-house, and introduced him to me.

'My cousin Julian—Miss Crofton.'

He bowed rather stiffly, and then seated himself by his cousin's side, and put his hat upon the table before him. I had plenty of time to look at him as he sat there talking of all sorts of things connected with Thornleigh, and Miss Darrell's friends in that neighbourhood. He was very good-looking, fair and pale, with regular well-cut features, and rather fine blue eyes; but I fancied those clear blue eyes had a cold look, and that there was an expression of iron will about the mouth and powerful prominent chin. The upper part of the face was thoughtful, and there were lines already on the high white forehead, from which the thin straight chestnut hair was carefully brushed. It was the face of a very clever man, I thought; but I was not so sure that it was the face of a man I could like, or whom I should be inclined to trust.

Mr. Stormont had a low pleasant voice and an agreeable manner of speaking. His way of treating his cousin was half deferential, half playful; but once, when I looked up suddenly from my work, I seemed to catch a glimpse of a deeper meaning in the cold blue eyes—a look of singular intensity fixed on Milly's bright face.

Whatever this look might mean, she was unconscious of it; she went on talking gaily of Thornleigh and her Thornleigh friends.

'I do so want to come home, Julian,' she said. 'Do you think there is any hope for me this midsummer?'

'I think there is every hope. I think it is almost certain you will come home.'

'O Julian, how glad I am!'

'But suppose there should be a surprise for you when you come home, Milly,—a change that you may not quite like, at first?'

'What change?'

'Has your father told you nothing?'

'Nothing, except about his journeys from place to place, and not much about them. He has written very seldom during the last six months.'

'He has been too much engaged, I suppose; and it's rather like him to have said nothing about it. How would you like a stepmother, Milly?'

She gave a little cry, and grew suddenly pale.

'Papa has married again!' she said.

Julian Stormont drew a newspaper from his pocket, and laid it before her, pointing to an announcement in one column:

'On May 18th, at the English legation in Paris, William Darrell, Esq., of Thornleigh, Yorkshire, to Augusta, daughter of the late Theodore Chester, Esq., of Regent's Park.'

He read this aloud very slowly, watching Milly's pale face as he read.

'There is no reason why this should distress you, my dear child,' he said. 'It was only to be expected that your father would marry again, sooner or later.'

'I have lost him!' she cried piteously.

'Lost him!'

'Yes; he can never be again the same to me that he has been. His new wife will come between us. No, Julian, I am not jealous. I do not grudge him his happiness, if this marriage can make him happy. I only feel that I have lost him for ever.'

'My dear Milly, that is utterly unreasonable. Your father told me most particularly to assure you of his unaltered affection, when I broke the news of this marriage to you. He was naturally a little nervous about doing it himself.'

'You must never let him know what I have said, Julian. He will never hear any expression of regret from me; and I will try to do my duty to this strange lady. Have you seen her yet?'

'No, they have not come home yet. They were in Switzerland when I heard of them last; but they are expected in a week or two. Come, my dear Milly, don't look so serious. I trust this marriage may turn out for your happiness, as well as for your father's. Rely upon it, you will find no change in his feelings towards you.'

'He will always be kind and good to me, I know,' she answered sadly. 'It is not possible for him to be anything but that; but I can never be his companion again as I have been. There is an end to all that.'

'That was a kind of association which could not be supposed to last all your life, Milly. It is to be hoped that somebody else will have a claim upon your companionship before many years have gone by.'

'I suppose you mean that I shall marry,' she said, looking at him with supreme indifference.

'Something like that, Milly.'

'I have always fancied myself living all my life with papa. I have never thought it possible that I could care for any one but him.'

Julian Stormont's face darkened a little, and he sat silent for some minutes, folding and refolding the newspaper in a nervous way.

'You are not very complimentary to your admirers at Thornleigh,' he said at last, with a short hoarse laugh.

'Who is there at Thornleigh? Have I really any admirers there?'

'I think I could name half-a-dozen.'

'Never mind them just now. I want you to tell me all you know about my stepmother.'

'That amounts to very little. All I can tell you is, that she is the daughter of a gentleman, highly accomplished, without money, and four-and-twenty years of age. She was travelling as companion to an elderly lady when your father met her in a picture-gallery at Florence. He knew the old lady, I believe, and by that means became acquainted with the younger one.'

'Only four-and-twenty! only four years older than I!'

'Rather young, is it not? but when a man of your father's age makes a second marriage, he is apt to marry a young woman. Of course this is quite a love-match.'

'Yes, quite a love-match,' Milly repeated, with a sigh.

I knew she could not help that natural pang of jealousy, as she thought how she and her father had once been all the world to each other. She had told me so often of their happy companionship, the perfect confidence that had existed between them.

Julian Stormont sat talking to her—and a little, a very little, to me—for about half an hour longer, and then departed. He was to sleep at Fendale, and go back to North Shields next morning. He was his uncle's right hand in the business, Milly told me; and from the little I had seen of him I could fancy him a power in any sphere.

'Papa has a very high opinion of him,' she said, when we were talking of him after he had left us.

'And you like him very much, I suppose?'

'O yes, I like him very well. I have known him all my life. We are almost like brother and sister; only Julian is one of those thoughtful reserved persons one does not get on with very fast.'

CHAPTER III

At Thornleigh

The midsummer holidays began at last, and Mr. Darrell came in person to fetch his daughter, much to her delight. She was not to return to school any more unless she liked, he told her. Her new mamma was most anxious to receive her, and she could have masters at Thornleigh to complete her education, if it were not already finished.

Her eyes were full of tears when she came to tell me this, and carry me off to the drawing-room to introduce me to her father, an introduction she insisted upon making in spite of my entreaties,—for I was rather shy at this period of my life, and dreaded an encounter with a stranger.

Mr. Darrell received me most graciously. He was a tall fine-looking man, very like the photograph in Milly's bedroom, and I detected the hard look about the mouth which I had noticed in both portraits. He seemed remarkably fond of his daughter; and I have never seen a prettier picture than she made as she stood beside him, clinging to his arm, and looking lovingly up at him with her dark hazel eyes.

He asked me where I was to spend my holidays; and on hearing that I was to stay at Albury Lodge, asked whether I would like to come to Thornleigh with Milly for the midsummer vacation. My darling clapped her hands gaily as he made this offer, and cried:

'O yes, Mary, you will come, won't you?—You dear kind papa, that is just like you, always able to guess what one wishes. There is nothing in the world I should like better than to have Mary at Thornleigh.'

'Then you have only to pack a box with all possible expedition, and to come away with us, Miss Crofton,' said Mr. Darrell; 'the train starts in an hour and a half. I can only give you an hour.'

I thanked him as well as I could—awkwardly enough, I daresay—for his kindness, and ran away to ask Miss Bagshot's consent to the visit. This she gave readily, in spite of some objections suggested by Miss Susan, and I had nothing more to do than to pack my few dresses— my two coloured muslins, a white dress for festive occasions, a black-silk dress which was preeminently my 'best,' and some print morning-dresses—wondering as I packed them how these things would pass current among the grandeurs of Thornleigh. All this was finished well within the hour, and I put my bonnet and shawl, and ran down— flushed with hurry and excitement, and very happy—to join my friends in the drawing-room.

Miss Bagshot was there, talking of her attachment to her sweet young friend, and her regret at losing her. Mr. Darrell cut these lamentations short when he found I was ready, and we drove off to the station in the fly that had brought him to Albury Lodge.

I looked at the little station to-day with a very different feeling from that dull despondency which had possessed me six months before, when I arrived there in the bleak January weather. The thought of five weeks' respite from the monotonous routine of Albury Lodge was almost perfect happiness. I did not forget those I loved at home, or cease to regret the poverty that prevented my going home for the holidays; but since this was impossible, nothing could have been pleasanter than the idea of the visit I was going to pay.

Throughout the journey Mr. Darrell was all that was gracious and kind. He talked a good deal of his wife; dwelling much upon her accomplishments and amiability, and assuring his daughter again and again that she could not fail to love her.

'I was a little bit of a coward in the business, I confess, Milly,' he said, in the midst of this talk, 'and hadn't courage to tell you anything till the deed was done; and then I thought it was as well to let Julian make the announcement.'

'You ought to have trusted me better, papa,' Milly said tenderly; and I knew what perfect self-abnegation there was in the happy smile with which she gave him her hand.

'And you are not angry with me, my darling?' he asked.

'Angry with you, papa? as if I had any right to be angry with you! Only try to love me a little, as you used to do, and I shall be quite happy.'

'I shall never love you less, my dear.'

The journey was not a long one; and the country through which we passed was very fair to look upon in the bright June afternoon. The landscape changed when we were within about thirty miles of our destination: the fertile farmlands and waving fields of green corn gave place to an open moor, and I felt from far off the fresh breath of the ocean. This broad undulating moorland was new to me, and I thought there was a wild kind of beauty in its loneliness. As for Milly, she looked out at the moor with rapture, and strained her eyes to catch the first glimpse of the hills about Thornleigh—those hills of which she had talked to me so often in her little room at school.

The station we had to stop at was ten miles from Mr. Darrell's house, and a barouche-and-pair was waiting for us in the sunny road outside. We drove along a road that crossed the moor, until we came to a little village of scattered houses, with a fine old church—at one end of which an ancient sacristy seemed mouldering slowly to decay. We drove past the gates of two or three rather important houses, lying half-hidden in their gardens, and then turned sharply off into a road that went up a hill, nearly at the top of which we came to a pair of noble old carved iron gates, surmounted with a coat-of-arms, and supported on each side by massive stone pillars, about which the ivy twined lovingly.

An old man came out of a pretty rustic-looking lodge and opened theses gates, and we drove through an avenue of some extent, which led straight to the front of the house, the aspect of which delighted me. It was very old and massively built, and had quite a baronial look, I thought. There was a wide stone terrace with ponderous moss-grown stone balustrades round three sides of it, and at each angle a broad flight of steps leading down to a second terrace, with sloping green banks that melted into the turf of the lawn. The house stood on the summit of a hill, and from one side commanded a noble view of the sea.

A lady came out of the curious old stone porch as the carriage drove up, and stood at the top of the terrace steps waiting for us. I guessed immediately that this must be Mrs. Darrell.

Milly hung back a little shyly, as her father led her up the steps with her hand through his arm. She was very pale, and I could see that she was trembling. Mrs. Darrell came forward to her quickly, and kissed her.

'My darling Emily,' she cried, 'I am so delighted to see you at last.—O William, you did not deceive me when you promised me a beautiful daughter.'

Milly blushed, and smiled at this compliment, but still clung to her father, with shy downcast eyes.

I had time to look at Mrs. Darrell while this introduction was being made. She was not by any means a beautiful woman, but she was what I suppose would have been called eminently interesting. She was tall and slim, very graceful-looking, with a beautiful throat and a well-shaped head. Her features, with the exception of her eyes, were in no way remarkable; but those were sufficiently striking to give character to a face that might otherwise have been insipid. They were large luminous gray eyes, with black lashes, and rather strongly-marked brows of a much darker brown than her hair. That was of a nondescript shade, neither auburn nor chestnut, and with little light or colour in its soft silky masses; but it seemed to harmonise very well with her pale complexion. Lavater has warned us to distrust any one whose hair and eyebrows are of a different colour. I remembered this as I looked at Mrs. Darrell.

She was dressed in white; and I fancied the transparent muslin, with no other ornament than a lilac ribbon at the waist, was peculiarly becoming to her slender figure and delicate face. Her husband seemed to think so too, for he looked at her with a fond admiring glance as he offered her his arm to return to the house.

'I mustn't forget to introduce Miss Crofton to you, Augusta,' he said; 'a school friend of Milly's, who has kindly accepted my invitation to spend the holidays with her.'

Mrs. Darrell gave me her hand; but I fancied that she did so rather coldly, and I had an uneasy sense that I was not very welcome to the new mistress of Thornleigh.

'You will find your old rooms all ready for you, Milly,' she said; 'I suppose we had better put Miss Crofton in the blue room—next yours?'

'If you please, Mrs. Darrell.'

'What, Milly, won't you call me mamma?'

Milly was silent for a few moments, with a pained expression in her face.

'Pray, forgive me,' she said in a low voice; 'I cannot call any one by that name.'

Augusta Darrell kissed her again silently.

'It shall be as you wish, dear,' she said, after a pause.

A rosy-cheeked, pleasant-looking girl, who had been accustomed to wait on Milly in the old time, came forward to meet us, and ran before us to our rooms, expressing her delight at her young lady's return all the way she went.

The rooms were very pretty, and were situated in that portion of the house which looked towards the sea. There was a sitting-room, brightly furnished with some light kind of wood, and with chintz hangings all over rose-buds and butterflies. This had been Milly's schoolroom, and there was a good many books in two pretty-looking bookcases on each side of the fireplace. Besides these, there were some curious old cabinets full of shells and china. It was altogether the prettiest, most homelike room one could imagine.

Opening out of this, there was a large airy bedroom, with three windows commanding that glorious view of moorland and sea; and beyond that, a dainty little dressing-room. The next door in the corridor opened into the room that had been allotted to me; a large comfortable-looking room, in which there was an old-fashioned mahogany four-post bed with blue-damask curtains.

I went to Milly's dressing-room when my own simple toilet was finished, and stood by the open window talking to her while she arranged her hair. She dismissed her little maid directly I went into the room, and I felt she had something to say to me.

'Well, Mary,' she began at once, 'what do you think of her?'

'Of Mrs. Darrell?'

'Of course.'

'What opinion can I possibly form about her, after seeing her for three minutes, Milly? I think she is very elegant-looking. That is the only idea I have about her yet.'

'Do you think she looks *true,* Mary? Do you think she has married papa because she loves him?'

'My dear child, how can I tell that? She is a great many years younger than your papa, but I do not see that the difference between them need be any real hindrance to her loving him. He is a man whom any woman might care for, I should think; to say nothing of her natural gratitude towards the man who has rescued her from a position of dependence.'

'Gratitude is all nonsense,' Miss Darrell answered impatiently. 'I want to know that my father is loved as he deserves to be loved. I shall never tolerate that woman unless I can feel sure of that.'

'I believe you are prejudiced against her already, Milly,' I said reproachfully.

'I daresay I am, Mary. I daresay I feel unjustly about her; but I don't like her face.'

'What is there in her face that you don't like?'

'O, I can't tell you that—an undefinable something. I have a sort of conviction that she and I can never love each other.'

'It is rather hard upon Mrs. Darrell to begin with such a feeling as that, Milly.'

'I can't help it. Of course I shall try to do my duty to her, for papa's sake, and I shall do my best to conquer all these unchristian feelings. But we cannot command our hearts, you know, Mary, and I don't think I shall ever love my stepmother.'

She took me down to the drawing-room after this. It was half-past six, and we were to dine at seven. The drawing-room was a long room, with five windows opening on to the terrace, an old-fashioned-looking room with panelled walls and a fine arched ceiling. The wainscot was painted white, with gilt mouldings, and the cornice and architraves of the doors were elaborately carved. The furniture was white-and-gold like the walls, and in that spurious classical style which prevailed during the first French Empire. The window-curtains and coverings of sofas and chairs were of dark-green velvet.

A gentleman was standing in one of the open windows looking out at the garden. He turned as Milly and I went in, and I recognised Mr. Stormont. He came forward to shake hands with his cousin, and smiled his peculiar slow smile at her expression of surprise.

'You didn't know I was here, Milly?'

'No, indeed; I had no idea of seeing you.'

'I wonder your father did not tell you of my visit. I came over this morning for a fortnight's holiday. I've been working a little harder than usual lately, and my uncle is good enough to say I have earned a rest.'

'I wonder you don't go abroad for a change.'

'I don't care about a change. I had much rather come to Thornleigh.'

He looked at her very earnestly as he said this. I had been sure of it that afternoon when we all three sat in the summer-house at Albury Lodge, but I could see that Milly herself had no idea of the truth.

'Well, Milly, what do you think of your new mamma?' he asked presently.

'I had rather not tell you yet.'

'Humph! that hardly sounds favourable to the lady. She seems to me a very charming person; but she is not my stepmother, and, of course, that makes a difference. Your father is intensely devoted.'

Mr. Darrell came into the room a few minutes after this, and his wife followed him almost immediately. Milly placed herself next her father, and contrived to absorb his attention, not quite to the satisfaction of the elder lady, I fancied. Those bright gray eyes flashed upon my darling with a brief look of anger, which changed in the next moment to quiet watchfulness.

Mrs. Darrell stood by one of the tables, idly turning over some books and papers, and finding me seated near her, began to talk to me presently in a very gracious manner, asking me how I liked Thornleigh, and a few other questions of a stereotyped kind; but even while she talked those watchful eyes were always turned towards the window where the father and daughter stood side by side. Mr. Stormont came over to her while she was talking to me, and joined in the conversation; in the midst of which a grave gray-haired old butler came to announce dinner.

Mr. Stormont offered his arm to the lady of the house, while Mr. Darrell gave one arm to me and the other to his daughter; and we went down a long passage, at the end of which was the dining-room, a noble old room, with dark oak panelling and a great many pictures by the old masters, which were, no doubt, as valuable as they were dingy. We dined at an oval table, prettily decorated with flowers and with some very curious old silver.

There was a good deal of talk at dinner, in which I could take very little part. Mr. and Mrs. Darrell talked to Julian Stormont of their travels; and I must confess the lady talked well, with no affectation of enthusiasm, and with an evident knowledge and appreciation of the things she was speaking about. I envied her those wanderings in sunny foreign lands, even though they had been made in the company of an invalid dowager, and I wondered whether she would be happy in a settled existence at Thornleigh.

After dinner Milly took me out upon the terrace, and from thence we went to explore the gardens. We had not been out long before Julian Stormont came to join us. We had been talking pleasantly enough till he appeared, but his coming seemed to make us both silent, and he himself had a thoughtful air. I watched his pale face as he walked beside us in the twilight, and was again struck by the careworn look about the brow and the resolute expression of the mouth.

He was very fond of Milly. Of that fact there could be no possible doubt; and I think he had already begun to suffer keenly from the knowledge that his love was unreturned. That he hoped against hope at this time— that he counted fully on his power to win her in the future, I know. He was too wise to precipitate matters by any untimely avowal of his feelings. He waited with a quiet resolute patience which was a part of his nature.

Of course we talked a little, but it was in a straggling, desultory kind of way; and I think it was a relief to all of us when we finished the round of the gardens and went in through one of the drawing-room windows. The room was lighted with lamps and candles placed about upon the tables, and Mrs. Darrell was sitting near her husband, employed upon some airy scrap of fancy-work, while he read his *Times*.

He asked for some music soon after we went in, and she rose to obey him with a very charming air of submission. She played magnificently, with a power and style that were quite new to me, for I had heard no professional performers. She sang an Italian scena afterwards, in a rich mezzo-soprano, and with a kind of suppressed passion that impressed me deeply. I scarcely wondered, after hearing her play and sing, that Mr. Darrell had been fascinated by her. These gifts of hers were in themselves sufficient to subjugate a man who really cared for music.

Milly was charmed into forgetfulness of her prejudices. She went over to the piano and kissed her stepmother.

'Papa told me how clever you were,' she said; 'but he did not tell me you were a genius.'

Mrs. Darrell received the compliment very modestly, and then tried to persuade Milly to sing or play; but the girl declined resolutely. Nothing could induce her to touch the piano after that brilliant performance.

The next day and several days passed very quietly, and in a kind of monotonous comfort. The rector of the parish dined with us one day, and on another a neighbouring squire with his wife and three daughters. Milly and I spent a good deal of our time in the gardens and on the sea-shore, with Julian Stormont for our companion, while Mr. and Mrs. Darrell rode or drove together. My darling could see that she was not expected to join them in these rides and drives, and I think this confirmed her idea that her father was in a manner lost to her.

'I must try to be satisfied with this new state of things, Mary,' she said, with a sigh of resignation. 'If my father is happy, I ought to be contented. But O, my dear, if you could have seen us together a year ago, you would know how much I have lost.'

I had been at Thornleigh a little more than a week, when Mr. Darrell one morning proposed a drive to a place called Cumber Priory, which was one of the show-houses of the neighbourhood. It was a very old place, he said, and had been one of the earliest monastic settlements in that part of the country. Milly and her father and her cousin had been there a great many times, and the visit was proposed for the gratification of Mrs. Darrell and myself.

She assented graciously, as she always did to every proposition of her husband's, and we started soon after breakfast in the barouche, with Julian Stormont on horseback. The drive was delightful; for, after leaving the hilly district about Thornleigh, our road lay through a wood, where the trees were of many hundred years' growth. I recognised groups of oak and beech that I had seen among the sketches in Milly's portfolio.

On the other side of the wood we came to some dilapidated-looking gates, with massive stone escutcheons on the great square pillars. There was a lodge, but it was evidently unoccupied, and Mr. Darrell's footman got down from the box to open the gates. Within we made the circuit of a neglected lawn, divided from a park by a sunk fence, across which some cattle stared at us in a lazy manner as we drove past them. The house was a long low building with heavily mullioned windows, and was flanked by gothic towers. Most of the windows had closed shutters, and the place had altogether a deserted look.

'The Priory has not been occupied for several years,' Mr. Darrell said, as if in answer to my thoughts as I looked up at the closed windows. 'The family have been too poor to live in it in anything like their old state. There is only one member of the old family remaining now, and he leads a wandering kind of life abroad, I believe.'

'What has made them so poor?' asked Mrs. Darrell.

'Extravagant habits, I suppose,' answered her husband, with an expressive shrug of the shoulders. 'The Egertons have always been a wild race.'

'Egerton!' Mrs. Darrell repeated; 'I thought the name of these people was Cumber.'

'No; Cumber is only the name of the place. It has been in the Egerton family for centuries.'

'Indeed!'

I was seated exactly opposite her, and I was surprised by the strange startled look in her face as she repeated the name of Egerton. That look passed away in the next moment, and left her with her usual air of languid indifference; a placid kind of listlessness which harmonised very well with her pale complexion and delicate features. She was not a woman from whom one expected much animation.

The low iron-studded door of the Priory was opened by a decent-looking old woman of that species which seems created expressly for the showing of old houses. She divined our errand at once, and as soon as we were in the hall, began her catalogue of pictures and curiosities in the usual mechanical way, while we looked about us, always fixing our eyes on the wrong object, and more bewildered than enlightened by her description of the chief features of the place.

We went from room to room, the dame throwing open the shutters of the deep-set gothic windows, and letting in a flood of sunshine upon the faded tapestries and tarnished picture-frames. It was a noble old place, and the look of decay upon everything was more in accord with its grandeur than any modern splendour could have been.

We had been through all the rooms on the ground floor, most of which opened into one another, and were returning towards the hall, when Mr. Darrell missed his wife, and sent me back to look for her in one direction, while he went in another. I hurried through three or four empty rooms, until I came to a small one at the end of the house, and here I found her. I had not noticed this room much, for it was furnished in a more modern style than the rest of the house, and the old housekeeper had made very light of it, hurrying us back to look at some armour over the chimneypiece in the next room. It was her master's study, she had said, and was not generally shown to strangers.

It was a small dark-looking room, lined with dingily-bound books upon heavy carved-oak shelves, and with no other furniture than a massive writing-table and three or four arm-chairs. Over the mantelpiece, which was modern and low, there was a portrait of a young man with a dark handsome face, and it was at this that Augusta Darrell was looking. I could see her face in profile as she stood upon the hearth with her clenched hand upon the mantelpiece, and I had never before seen such an expression in any human countenance.

What was it? Despair, remorse, regret? I know not; but it was a look of keenest anguish, of unutterable sorrow. The face was deadly pale, the great gray eyes looking upwards at the portrait, the lips locked together rigidly.

She did not hear my footstep; it was only when I spoke to her that she turned towards me with a stony face, and asked what I wanted.

I told her that Mr. Darrell had sent me.

'I was coming this instant,' she said, resuming her usual manner with an effort. 'I had only loitered to look at that portrait. A fine face, is it not, Miss Crofton?'

'A handsome one, at any rate,' I answered doubtfully, for that dark haughty countenance struck me as rather repellent than attractive.

'That's as much as to say you don't think it a good face. Well, perhaps you are right. It reminded me of some one I knew a long time ago, and was rather interesting to me on that account. And then I fell into a kind of a reverie, and forgot that my dear husband might miss me.'

He came into the room as she was saying this. She told him that she had stopped to look at the portrait, and asked whose it was.

'It is a likeness of Angus Egerton, the present owner of the Priory,' Mr. Darrell answered; 'and a very good likeness, too—of as bad a man as ever lived, I believe,' he added in a lower voice.

'A bad man?'

'Yes; he broke his mother's heart.'

'In what manner?'

'He fell in love with a girl of low birth, whom he met in the course of a pedestrian tour in the West of England, and was going to marry her, I believe, when Mrs. Egerton got wind of the affair. She was a very proud woman—one of the most resolute masculine-minded women I ever knew. She went down into Devonshire where the girl lived immediately, and by some means or other prevented the marriage. How it was done I never heard; but it was not until a year afterwards that Angus Egerton discovered his mother's part in the business. He came down to the Priory suddenly and unexpectedly at a late hour one night, and walked straight to his mother's room. I have heard that old woman who has been showing us the house describe his ghastly face—she was Mrs. Egerton's maid in those days—as he pushed her aside and went into the room where his mother was sitting. There was a dreadful scene between them, and at the end of it Angus Egerton walked out of the house, swearing never again to enter it while his mother lived. He has kept his word. Mrs. Egerton never crossed the threshold after that night, and refused to see anybody except her servants and her doctor. She lived this lonely kind of life for nearly three years, and then died of some slow wasting disease, for which the doctor could find no name.'

'And where did Mr. Egerton go after leaving her that night?'

'He slept at a little inn at Cumber, and went back to London next morning. He left England soon after that, and has lived abroad ever since.'

'And you think him a very bad man?'

'I consider his conduct to his mother a sufficient evidence of that.'

'He may have believed himself deeply wronged.'

'He must have known that she had acted in his interests when she prevented his committing the folly of a low marriage. She was his mother, and had been a most devoted and indulgent mother.'

'And in the end contrived to break his heart—to say nothing of the girl who loved him, who was of course a piece of common clay, not worth consideration.'

'I did not think you had so much romance, Augusta,' said Mr. Darrell, laughing; 'I suppose it is natural for a woman to take the part of unfortunate lovers, however foolish the affair may be. But I believe this Devonshire girl was quite unworthy of an honourable attachment on the part of any man. You see I knew and liked Mrs. Egerton, and I know how she loved her son. I cannot forgive him his conduct to her; nor have the reports of his life abroad been by any means favourable to his character. His career seems to have been a very wild and dissipated one.'

'And he has never married?'

'No, he has never married.'

'He has been true, at least,' Mrs. Darrell said in a low thoughtful tone.

We had lingered in the little study while her husband had told his story. We went back to the hall now, and found Milly and Mr. Stormont looking rather listlessly at the old portraits of the Egerton race. I was anxious to see a picture of the last Mrs. Egerton, after what I had heard about her, and, at my request, the housekeeper showed me one in the drawing-room.

She was very handsome, and wonderfully like her son. I could fancy those two haughty spirits in opposition.

We spent another hour looking over the rest of the house— old tapestry, old pictures, old china, old furniture, secret staircases, carved chimneypieces, muniment chests, and the usual objects of interest to be found in such a place. After that we walked a little in the neglected garden, where there were old holly hedges that had grown high and wild for want of clipping, and where a curious old sun-dial had fallen down upon the grass in a forlorn way. The paths were all green and moss-grown, and the roses were almost choked with bindweed. I saw Mrs. Darrell gather one of these roses and put it in her breast. It was the first time I have ever seen her pluck a flower, though there was a wealth of roses at Thornleigh.

So ended our visit to Cumber Priory; a place that was destined to be very memorable to some of us in the time to come.

CHAPTER IV

Mrs. Thatcher

It had been Milly's habit to devote one day a week to visiting among the poor, before she went to Albury Lodge; and she now resumed this practice, I accompanying her upon her visits. I had been used to going about among the cottagers at home, and I liked the work. It was very pleasant to see Milly Darrell with these people—the perfect confidence and sympathy between them and her, the delight they seemed to take in her bright cheering presence. I was struck by their simple natural manner, and the absence of anything like sycophancy to be observed in them. One day, when we had been to several cottages about the village, Milly asked me if I could manage rather a long walk; and on my telling her that I could, we started upon a lonely road that wound across the moor in a direction I had never walked in until that day. We went on for about two miles without passing a human habitation, and then came to one of the most desolate-looking cottages I ever remember seeing. It was little better than a cabin, and consisted only of two rooms—a kind of kitchen or dwelling-room, and a dark little bedchamber opening out of it.

'I am not going to introduce you to a very agreeable person, Mary,' Milly said, when we were within a few paces of this solitary dwelling; 'but old Rebecca is a character in her way, and I make a point of coming to see her now and then, though she is not always very gracious to me.'

It was a warm bright summer's day, but the door and the single window of the cottage were firmly closed. Milly knocked with her hand, and a thin feeble old voice called to her to 'come in.'

We went in: the atmosphere of the place was hot, and had an unpleasant doctor's-shoppish kind of odour, which I found was caused by some herbs in a jar that was simmering over a little stove in a corner. Bunches of dried herbs hung from the low ceiling, and on an old-fashioned lumbering chest of drawers that stood in the window there were more herbs and roots laid out to dry.

'Mrs. Thatcher is a very clever doctor, Mary,' said Milly, as if by way of introduction; 'all our servants come to her to be cured when they have colds and coughs.— And how are you this lovely summer weather, Mrs. Thatcher?'

'None too well, miss,' grumbled the old woman; 'I don't like the summer time; it never suited me.'

'That's strange,' said Milly gaily; 'I thought everybody liked summer.'

'Not those that live as I do, Miss Darrell. There's no illness in summer—no colds, nor coughs, nor sore-threats, nor suchlikes. I don't know that I shouldn't starve outright, if it wasn't for the ague; and even that is nothing now to what it used to be.'

I was quite horror-struck by this ghoulish speech; but Milly only laughed gaily at the old woman's candour.

'If the doctors were as plain-spoken as you, I daresay they'd say pretty much the same kind of thing, Mrs. Thatcher,' she said. 'How's your grandson?'

'O, he's well enough, Miss Darrell. Naught's never in danger.—Peter, come here, and see the young ladies.'

A poor, feeble, pale-faced, semi-idiotic-looking boy came slowly out of the dark little bedroom, and stood grinning at us. He had the white sickly aspect of a creature reared without the influence of air and light; and I pitied him intensely as he stood there staring and grinning in that dreadful hopeless manner.

'Poor Peter!' He's no better, I'm afraid,' said Milly gently.

'No, miss, nor never will be. He knows more than people think, and has queer cunning ways of his own; but he'll never be any better or wiser than he is now.'

'Not if you were to take as much pains with him as you do with the patients who pay you, Mrs. Thatcher?' asked Milly.

'I've taken pains with him,' answered the woman, with a scowl. 'I took to him kindly enough when he was a little fellow; but he's grown up to be nothing but a plague and a burden to me.'

The boy left off grinning, and his poor weak chin sank lower on his narrow chest. His attitude had been a stooping one from the first; but he drooped visibly under the old woman's reproof.

'Can he employ himself in no way?'

'No, miss; except in picking the herbs and roots for me sometimes. He can do that, and he knows one from t'other.'

'He's of some use to you, at any rate, then,' said Milly.

'Little enough,' the old woman answered sulkily. 'I don't want help; I've plenty of time to gather them myself. But I've taught him to pick them, and it's the only thing he ever could learn.'

'Poor fellow! He's your only grandchild, isn't he, Mrs. Thatcher?'

'Yes, he's the only one, miss, and he'd need be. I don't know how I should keep another. You can't remember my daughter Ruth? She was as pretty a girl as you'd care to see. She was housemaid at Cumber priory in Mrs. Egerton's time, and she married the butler. They set up in business in a little public-house in Thornleigh village, and he took to drinking, till everything went to rack and ruin. My poor girl took the trouble to heart more than her husband did, a great deal; and I believe it was the trouble that killed her. She died three weeks after that boy was born, and her husband ran away the day after the funeral, and has never been heard of since. Some say he drowned himself in the Clem; but he was a precious deal too fond of himself for that. He was up to his eyes in debt, and didn't leave a sixpence behind him; that's how Peter came to be thrown on my hands.'

'Come here, Peter,' said Milly softly; and the boy went to her directly, and took the hand she offered him.

'You've not forgotten me, have you, Peter? Miss Darrell, who used to talk to you sometimes a long time ago.'

The boy's vacant face brightened into something like intelligence.

'I know you, miss,' he said; 'you was always kind to Peter. It's not many that I know; but I know you.'

She took out her purse and gave him half-a-crown.

'There, Peter, there's a big piece of silver for your own self, to buy whatever you like—sugar-sticks, ginger-bread, marbles—anything.'

His clumsy hand closed upon the coin, and I have no doubt he was pleased by the donation; but he never took his eyes from Milly Darrell's face. That bright lovely face seemed to exercise a kind of fascination upon him.

'Don't you think Peter would be better if you were to give him a little more air and sunshine, Mrs. Thatcher?' Milly asked presently; 'that bedroom seems rather a dark close place.'

'He needn't be there unless he likes,' Mrs. Thatcher answered indifferently. 'He sits out of doors whenever he chooses.'

'Then I should always sit out-of-doors on fine days, if I were you, Peter,' said Milly.

After this she talked a little to Mrs. Thatcher, who was by no means a sympathetic person, while I sat looking on, and contemplating the old woman with a feeling that was the reverse of admiration.

She was of a short squat figure, with broad shoulders and no throat to speak of, and her head seemed too big for her body. Her face was long and thin, with large features, and a frame of scanty gray hair, among which a sandy tinge still lingered here and there; her eyes were of an ugly reddish-brown, and had, I thought, a most sinister expression. I must have been very ill, and sorely at a loss for a doctor, before I could have been induced to trust my health to the care of Mrs. Rebecca Thatcher.

I told Milly as much while we were walking homewards, and she admitted that Rebecca Thatcher was no favourite even among the country people, who believed implicitly in her skill.

'I'm afraid she tells fortunes, and dabbles in all sorts of superstitious tricks,' Milly added gravely; 'but she is so artful, there is no way of finding her out in that kind of business. The foolish country girls who consult her always keep her secret, and she manages to put on a fair face before our rector and his curate, who believe her to be a respectable woman.'

The days and weeks slipped by very pleasantly at Thornleigh, and the end of those bright midsummer holidays came only too soon. It seemed a bitter thing to say 'good-bye' to Milly Darrell, and to go back alone to a place which must needs be doubly dull and dreary to me without her. She had been my only friend at Albury Lodge; loving her as I did, I had never cared to form any other friendship.

The dreaded day came at last—dreaded I know by both of us; and I said 'good-bye' to my darling so quietly, that I am sure none could have guessed the grief I felt in this parting. Mrs. Darrell was very kind and gracious on this occasion, begging that I would come back to Thornleigh at Christmas—if they should happen to spend their Christmas there.

Milly looked up at her wonderingly as she said this.

'Is there any chance of our spending it elsewhere, Augusta?' she asked.

Mrs. Darrell had persuaded her stepdaughter to use this familiar Christian name, rather than the more formal mode of address.

'I don't know, my dear. Your papa has sometimes talked of a house in town, or we might be abroad. I can only say that if we are at home here, we shall be very much pleased to see Miss Crofton again.'

I thanked her, kissed Milly once more, and so departed—to be driven to the station in state in the barouche, and to look sadly back at the noble old house in which I had been so happy.

Once more I returned to the dryasdust routine of Albury Lodge, and rang the changes upon history and geography, chronology and English grammar, physical science and the elements of botany, until my weary head ached and my heart grew sick. And when I came to be a governess, it would of course be the same thing over and over again, on a smaller scale. And this was to be my future, without hope of change or respite, until I grew an old woman worn-out with the drudgery of tuition!

CHAPTER V

Milly's Letter

The half-year wore itself slowly away. There were no incidents to mark the time, no change except the slow changes of the seasons; and my only pleasures were letters from home or from Emily Darrell.

Of the home letters I will not speak—they could have no interest except for myself; but Milly's are links in the story of a life. She wrote to me as freely as she had talked to me, pouring out all her thoughts and fancies with that confiding frankness which was one of the most charming attributes of her mind. For some time the letters contained nothing that could be called news; but late in September there came one which seemed to me to convey intelligence of some importance.

'You will be grieved to hear, my darling Mary,' she wrote, after a little playful discussion of my own affairs, 'that my stepmother and I are no nearer anything like a real friendship than we were when you left us. What it is that makes the gulf between us, I cannot tell; but there is something, some hidden feeling in both our minds, I think, which prevents our growing fond of each other. She is very kind to me, so far as perfect non-interference with my doings, and a gracious manner when we are together, can go; but I am sure she does not like me. I have surprised her more than once looking at me with the strangest expression—a calculating, intensely thoughtful look, that made her face ten years older than it is at other times. Of course there are times when we are thrown together alone—though this does not occur often, for she and my father are a most devoted couple, and spend the greater part of every day together—and I have noticed at those times that she never speaks of her girlhood, or of any part of her life before her marriage. All that came before seems a blank page, or a sealed volume that she does not care to open. I asked some trifling question about her father once, and she turned upon me almost angrily.

"I do not care to speak about him, Milly," she said; "he was not a good father, and he is best forgotten. I never had a real friend till I met my husband."

'There is one part of her character which I am bound to appreciate. I believe that she is really grateful and devoted to papa, and he certainly seems thoroughly happy in her society. The marriage had the effect which I felt sure it must have—it has divided us two most completely; but if it has made him happy, I have no reason to complain. What could I wish for beyond his happiness?

'And now, Milly, for my news. Julian Stormont has been here, and has asked me to be his wife.

'He came over last Saturday afternoon, intending to stop with us till Monday morning. It was a bright warm day here, and in the afternoon he persuaded me to walk to Cumber Church with him. You remember the way we drove through the wood the day we went to the Priory, I daresay; but there is a nearer way than that for foot passengers, and I think a prettier one—a kind of cross-cut through the same wood. I consented willingly enough, having nothing better to do with myself, and we had a pleasant walk to church, talking of all kinds of things. As we returned Julian grew very serious, and when we were about half way upon our journey, he asked me if I could guess what had brought him over to Thornleigh. Of course I told him that I concluded he had come as he usually did—for rest and change after the cares of business, and to talk about business affairs with papa.

'He told me he had come for something more than that. He came to tell me that he had loved me all his life; that there was nothing my father would like better than our union if it could secure my happiness, as he hoped and believed it might.

'I think you know, Mary, that no idea of this kind had ever entered my mind. I told Julian this, and told him that, however I might esteem him as my cousin, he could never be nearer or dearer to me than that. The change in his face when he heard this almost frightened me. He grew deadly pale, but I am certain it was anger rather than disappointment that was uppermost in his mind. I never knew until then what a hard cruel face it could be.

"Is this irrevocable, Emily?" he asked, in a cold firm voice; "is there no hope that you will change your mind by and by?"

"No, Julian; I am never likely to do that."

"There is some one else, then, I suppose," he said.

"No, indeed, there is no one else."

"Highly complimentary to me!" he cried, with a harsh laugh.

'I was very sorry for him, in spite of that angry look.

"Pray don't imagine that I do not appreciate your many high qualities, Julian," I said, "or that I do not feel honoured by your preference for me. No doubt there are many women in the world better deserving your regard than I am, who would be able to return it."

"Thank you for that little conventional speech," he cried with a sneer. "A man builds all his hopes of happiness on one woman, and she coolly shatters the fabric of his life, and then tells him to go and build elsewhere. I daresay there are women in the world who would condescend to marry me if I asked them, but it is my misfortune to care only for one woman. I can't transfer my affection, as a man transfers his capital from one form of investment to another."

'We walked on for some time in silence. I was determined not to be angry with him, however ungraciously he might speak to me; and when we were drawing near home, I begged that we might remain friends still, and that this unfortunate conversation might make no difference between us. I told him I knew how much my father valued him, and that it would distress me deeply if he deserted Thornleigh on my account.

"Friends!" he replied, in an absent tone; "yes, we are still friends of course, and I shall not desert Thornleigh."

'He seemed gayer than usual that evening after dinner. Whether the gaiety was assumed in order to hide his depression, or whether he was really able to take the matter lightly, I cannot tell. Of course I cannot shut out of my mind the consideration that a marriage with me would be a matter of great worldly advantage to Julian, who has nothing but the salary he receives from my father, and who by such a marriage would most likely secure immediate possession of the business, in which he is already a kind of deputy principal.

'I noticed that my stepmother was especially kind to Julian this evening, and that she and he sat apart in one of the windows for some time talking to each other in a low confidential tone, while my father took his after-dinner nap. I wonder whether he told her of our interview that afternoon?

'He went back to Shields early next morning, and bade me good-bye quite in his usual manner; so I hoped he had forgiven me; but the affair has left an unpleasant feeling in my mind, a sort of vague dread of some trouble to arise out of it in the future. I cannot forget that hard cruel look in my cousin's face.

'When he was gone, Mrs. Darrell began to praise him very warmly, and my father spoke of him in the same tone. They talked of him a good deal as we lingered over our breakfast, and I fancied there was some intention with regard to me in the minds of both—they seem indeed to think alike upon every subject. Dearly as I love my father, this is a point upon which even his influence could not affect me. I might be weak and yielding upon every other question, never upon this.

'And now let me tell you about my friend Peter, Rebecca Thatcher's half-witted grandson. You know how painfully we were both struck by the poor fellow's listless hopeless manner when we were at the cottage on the moor. I thought of it a great deal afterwards, and it occurred to me that our head-gardener might find work for him in the way of weeding, and rolling the gravel paths, and such humble matters. Brook is a good kind old man, and always ready to do anything to please me; so I asked him the question one day in August, and he promised that when he next wanted extra hands Peter Thatcher should be employed, "Though I don't suppose I shall ever make much of him, miss," he said; "but there's naught I wouldn't do to please you."

'Well, my dear Mary, the boy came, and has done so well as quite to surprise Brook and the other two gardeners. He has an extraordinary attachment to me, and nothing delights him so much as to wait upon me when I am attending to my ferns, a task I always perform myself, as you know. To see this poor boy, standing by with a watering-pot in one hand, and a little basket of dead leaves in the other, watching me as breathlessly as if I were some great surgeon operating upon a patient, would make you smile; but I think you could scarcely fail to be touched by his devotion. He tells me that he is so happy at Thornleigh, and he begins to look a great deal brighter already. The men say he is indefatigable in his work, and worth two ordinary boys. He is passionately fond of flowers, and I have begun to teach him the elements of botany. It is rather slow work impressing the names of the plants upon his poor feeble brain; but he is so anxious to learn, and so proud of being taught, that I am well repaid for my trouble.'

Milly was very anxious that I should spend Christmas at Thornleigh; but it was by that time nearly a year since I had seen the dear ones at home, and ill as my dear father could afford any addition to his expenses, he wished me to spend my holidays with him; and so it was arranged that I should return to Warwickshire, much to my dear girl's regret.

The holiday was a very happy one; and, before it was over, I received a letter from Milly, telling me that Mr. and Mrs. Darrell were going abroad for some months, and asking me to cut short my term at Albury Lodge, and come to Thornleigh as her companion, at a salary which I thought a very handsome one.

The idea of exchanging the dull monotony of Miss Bagshot's establishment for such a home as Thornleigh, with the friend I loved as dearly as a sister, was more than delightful to me, to say nothing of a salary which would enable me to buy my own clothes and leave a margin for an annual remittance to my father. I talked the subject over with him, and he wrote immediately to Miss Bagshot, requesting her to waive the half-year's notice of the withdrawal of my services, to which she was fairly entitled. This she consented very kindly to do; and instead of going back to Albury Lodge, I went to Thornleigh.

Mr. and Mrs. Darrell had started for Paris when I arrived, and the house seemed very empty and quiet. My dear girl came into the hall to receive me, and led me off to her pretty sitting-room, where there was a bright fire, and where, she told me, she spent almost the whole of her time now.

'And are you really pleased to come to me, Mary?' she asked, when our first greetings were over.

'More than pleased, my darling. It seems almost too bright a life for me. I can hardly believe in it yet.'

'But perhaps you will seen get as tired of Thornleigh as ever you did of Albury Lodge. It will be rather a dull kind of life, you know; only you and I and the old servants.'

'I shall never feel dull with you, Milly. But tell me how all this came about. How was it you didn't go abroad with Mr. and Mrs. Darrell?'

'Ah, that is rather strange, isn't it? The truth of the matter is, that Augusta did not want me to go with them. She does not like me, Mary, that is the real truth, through she affects to be very fond of me, and has contrived to make my father think she is so. What is there that she cannot make him think? She does not like me; and she is never quite happy or at her ease when I am with her. She had been growing tired of Thornleigh for some time when the winter began; and she looked so pale and ill, that my father got anxious about her. The doctor here treated her in the usual stereotyped way, and made very light of her ailments, but recommended change of air and scene. Papa proposed going to Scarborough; but somehow or other Augusta contrived to change Scarborough into Paris, and they are to spend the winter and spring there, and perhaps go on to Germany in the summer. At first papa was very anxious to take me with them; but Augusta dropped some little hints—it would interrupt my studies, and unsettle me, and so on. You know I am rather proud, Mary, so you can imagine I was not slow to understand her. I said I would much prefer to stay at Thornleigh, and proposed immediately that you should come to me and be my companion, and help me on with my studies.'

'My dearest, how good of you to wish that!'

'It was not at all good. I think you are the only person in the world who really cares for me, now that I have lost papa—for I have lost him, you see, Mary; that becomes more obvious every day. Well, dear, I had a hard battle to fight. Mrs. Darrell said you were absurdly young for such a position, and that I required a matronly person, able to direct and protect me, and take the management of the house in her absence, and so on; but I said that I wanted neither direction nor protection; that the house wanted no other management than that of Mrs. Bunce the housekeeper, who has managed it ever since I was a baby; and that if I could not have Mary Crofton, I would have no one at all. I told papa what an indefatigable darling you were, and how conscientiously you would perform anything you promised to do. So, after a good deal of discussion, the matter was settled; and here we are, with the house all to ourselves, and the prospect of being alone together for six months to come.'

I asked her if she had seen much of Mr. Stormont since that memorable Sunday afternoon.

'He has been here twice,' she said, 'for his usual short visit from Saturday afternoon till Monday morning, and he has treated me just as if that uncomfortable interview had never taken place.'

We were very happy together in the great lonely house, amongst old servants, who seemed to take a pleasure in waiting on us. We spent our mornings and evenings in Milly's sitting-room, and took our meals in a snug prettily-furnished breakfast-room on the ground-floor. We read together a great deal, going through a systematic course of study of a very different kind from the dry labours at Albury Lodge. There was a fine old library at Thornleigh, and we read the masters of English and French prose together with unflagging interest and pleasure. Besides all this, Milly worked hard at her music, and still harder at her painting, which was a real delight to her.

Mr. Collingwood the rector, and his family, came to see us, and insisted on our visiting them frequently in a pleasant unceremonious manner; and we had other invitations from Milly's old friends in the neighbourhood of Thornleigh.

There were carriages at our disposal, but we did not often use them. Milly preferred walking; and we used to take long rambles together whenever the weather was favourable—rambles across the moor, or far away over the hills, or deep into the wood between Thornleigh and Cumber.

CHAPTER VI

A New Acquaintance

It was shortly after my arrival at Thornleigh that I first saw the man whose story I had heard in the study at Cumber Priory. Milly and I had been together about a fortnight, and it was the end of January—cold, clear, bright weather—when we set out early one afternoon for a ramble in our favourite wood, Milly furnished with pencils and sketch-book, in order to jot down any striking effect of the gaunt leafless old trees. She had a hardy disregard of cold in her devotion to her art, and would sit down to sketch in the bitter January weather in spite of my entreaties.

We stayed out longer than usual, and Milly had stopped once or twice to make a hasty sketch, when the sky grew suddenly dark, and big drops of rain began to fall slowly. There were speedily succeeded by a pelting storm of rain and hail, and we felt that we were caught, and must be drenched to the skin before we could get back to Thornleigh. The weather had been temptingly fine when we left home, and we had neither umbrellas nor any other kind of protection against the rain.

'We had better scamper off as fast as we can,' said Milly.

'But we can't run four miles. Hadn't we better go on to Cumber, and wait in the village till the weather changes, or try to get some kind of conveyance there?'

'Well, I suppose that would be best. There must be such a thing as a fly at Cumber, I should think, small as the place is. But it's nearly a mile from here to the village.'

'Anything seems better than going back through the wood in such a weather,' I said.

We were close to the outskirts of the wood at this time, and within a very short distance of the Priory gates. While we were still pausing in an undecided way, with the rain pelting down upon us, a figure came towards us from among the leafless trees—the figure of a man, a gentleman, as we could see by his dress and bearing, and a stranger. We had never met any one but country-people, farm-labourers, and so on, in the wood before, and were a little startled by his apparition.

He came up to us quickly, lifting his hat as he approached us.

'Caught in the storm, ladies,' he said, 'and without umbrellas I see, too. Have you far to go?'

'Yes, we have to go as far as Thornleigh,' Milly answered.

'Quite impossible in such weather. Will you come into the Priory and wait till the storm is over?'

'The Priory! To be sure!' cried Milly. 'I never thought of that. I know the housekeeper very well, and I am sure she would let us stop there.'

We walked towards the Priory gates, the stranger accompanying us. I had no opportunity of looking at him under that pelting rain, but I was wondering all the time who he was, and how he came to speak of Cumber Priory in that familiar tone.

One of the gates stood open, and we went in.

'A desolate-looking place, isn't it?' said the stranger. 'Dismal enough, without the embellishment of such weather as this.'

He led the way to the hall-door, and opened it unceremoniously, standing aside for us to pass in before him. There was a fire burning in the wide old-fashioned fireplace, and the place had an air of occupation that was new to it.

'I'll send for Mrs. Mills, and she shall take your wet shawls away to be dried,' said the stranger, ringing a bell; and I think we both began to understand by this time that he must be the master of the house.

'You are very kind,' Milly answered, taking off her dripping shawl. 'I did not know that the Priory was occupied except by the old servants. I fear you must have thought me very impertinent just now when I talked so coolly of taking shelter here.'

'I am only too glad that you should find refuge in the old place.'

He wheeled a couple of ponderous carved-oak chairs close to the hearth, and begged us to sit there; but Milly preferred standing in the noble old gothic window looking out at the rain.

'They will be getting anxious about us at home,' she said, 'if we are not back before dark.'

'I wish I possessed a close carriage to place at your service. I do, indeed, boast of the ownership of a dog-cart,

if you would not be afraid of driving in such a barba-
rous vehicle when the rain is over. It would keep you
out of the mud, at any rate.'

Milly laughed gaily.

'I have been brought up in the country,' she said, 'and
am not at all afraid of driving in a dog-cart. I used often to go out with papa in his, before he married.'

'Then, when the storm is over, I shall have the pleasure
of driving you to Thornleigh, if you will permit me that
honour.'

Milly looked a little perplexed at this, and made some
excuse about not wishing to cause so much trouble.

'I really think we could walk home very well; don't you,
Mary?' she said; and I declared myself quite equal to
the walk.

'It would be impossible for you to get back to Thornleigh before dark,' the gentleman remonstrated. 'I shall
be quite offended if you refuse the use of my dog-cart,
and insist on getting wet feet. I daresay your feet are
wet as it is, by the bye.'

We assured him of the thickness of our boots, and gave
our shawls to Mrs. Mills the old housekeeper, who carried them off to be dried in the kitchen, and promised
to convey the order about the dog-cart to the stables
immediately.

I had time now to look at our new acquaintance, who
was standing with his shoulders against one angle of
the high oak mantelpiece, watching the rain beating
against a window opposite to him. I had no difficulty in
recognising the original of that portrait which Augusta
Darrell had looked at so strangely. He was much older

than when the portrait had been taken—ten years at the least, I thought. In the picture he looked little more than twenty, and I should have guessed him now to be on the wrong side of thirty.

He was handsome still, but the dark powerful face had a sort of rugged look, the heavy eyebrows overshadowed the sombre black eyes, a thick fierce-looking moustache shrouded the mouth, but could not quite conceal an expression, half cynical, half melancholy, that lurked about the lowered corners of the full firm lips. He looked like a man whose past life held some sad or sinful history.

I could fancy, as I looked at him, that last bitter interview with his mother, and I could imagine how hard and cruel such a man might be under the influence of an unpardonable wrong. Like Mrs. Darrell, I was inclined to place myself on the side of the unfortunate lovers, rather than on that of the mother, who had been willing to sacrifice her son's happiness to her pride of race.

We all three remained silent for some little time, Milly and I standing together in the window, Mr. Egerton leaning against the mantelpiece, watching the rain with an absent look in his face. He roused himself at last, as if with an effort, and came over to the window by which we stood.

'It looks rather hopeless at present,' he said; 'but I shall spin you over to Thornleigh in no time; so you mustn't be anxious. It is at Thornleigh Manor you live, is it not?'

'Yes,' Milly answered. 'My name is Darrell, and this young lady is Miss Crofton, my very dear friend.'

He bowed in recognition of this introduction.

'I thought as much—I mean as to your name being Darrell. I had the honour to know Mr. Darrell very well when I was a lad, and I have a vague recollection of a small child in white frock, who, I think, must have been yourself. I have only been home a week, or I should have done myself the pleasure of calling on your father.'

'Papa is in Paris,' Milly answered, 'with my stepmother.'

'Ah, he has married again, I hear. One of the many changes that have come to pass since I was last in Yorkshire.'

'Have you returned for good, Mr. Egerton?'

'For good—or for evil—who knows?' he answered, with a careless laugh. 'As to whether I stay here so many weeks or so many years, that is a matter of supreme uncertainty. I never am in the same mind very long together. But I am heartily sick of knocking about abroad, and I cannot possibly find life emptier or duller here than I have found it in places that people call gay.'

'I can't fancy any one growing tired of such a place as the Priory,' said Milly.

' "Stone walls do not a prison make, nor iron bars a cage." " 'Tis in ourselves that we are thus or thus." Cannot you fancy a man getting utterly tired of himself and his own thoughts—knowing himself by heart, and finding the lesson a dreary one? Perhaps not. A girl's life seems all brightness. What should such happy young creatures know of that arid waste of years that lies beyond a man's thirtieth birthday, when his youth has not been a fortunate one? Ah, there is a break in the sky yonder; the rain will be over presently.'

The rain did cease, as he had prophesied. The dog-cart was brought round to the door by a clumsy-looking man in corduroy, who seemed half groom, half garden-er; and Mr. Egerton drove us home; Milly sitting next him, I at the back. His horse was very good one, and the drive only lasted a quarter of an hour, during which time our new acquaintance talked very pleasantly to both of us.

I could not forget that Mr. Darrell had called him a bad man; but in spite of that sweeping condemnation I could not bring myself to think of him without a cer-tain interest.

Of course Milly and I discussed Mr. Egerton as we sat over our snug little *tete-a-tete* dinner, and we were both inclined to speak of his blighted life in a pitying kind of way, and to blame his mother's conduct, little as we knew of the details of the story. Our existences were so quiet that this little incident made quite an event, and we were apt to date things from that afternoon for some time afterwards.

CHAPTER VII

A Little Match-Making

We heard nothing of Mr. Egerton for about three weeks, at the end of which time we were invited to dine at the Rectory. The first person we saw on going into the long, low, old-fashioned drawing-room was the master of Cumber Priory leaning against the mantelpiece in his favourite attitude. The Rector was not in the room when we arrived, and Angus Egerton was talking to Mrs. Collingwood, who sat in a low chair near the fire.

'Mr. Egerton has been telling me about your adventure in the wood, Milly,' Mrs. Collingwood said, as she rose to receive us. 'I hope it will be a warning to you to be more careful in future. I think that Cumber Wood is altogether too dangerous a place for two young ladies like you and Miss Crofton.'

'The safest place in the world,' cried Angus Egerton. 'I shall always be at hand to come to the ladies' assistance, and shall pray for the timely appearance of an infuriated bull, in order that I may distinguish myself by something novel in the way of a rescue. I hear that you are a very charming artist, Miss Darrell, and that you have done some of our oaks and beeches the honour to immortalise them.'

There is no need for me to record all the airy empty talk of that evening. It was a very pleasant evening. Angus Egerton had received his first lessons in the classics from the kind old Rector, and had been almost a son of the house in the past, the girls told me. He had resumed his old place upon his return, and seemed really fond of these friends, whom he had found ready to welcome him warmly in spite of all rumours to his disadvantage that had floated to Thornleigh during the years of his absence.

He was very clever, and seemed to have been everywhere, and to have seen everything worth seeing that the world contained. He had read a great deal too, in spite of his wandering life; and the fruit of his reading cropped up pleasantly now and then in his conversation.

There were no other guests, except an old country squire, who talked of nothing but his farming. Milly sat next Angus Egerton; and from my place on the other side of the table I could see how much she was interested in his talk. He did not stop long in the dining-room after we had left, but joined us as we sat round the fire in the drawing-room, talking over the poor people with Mrs. Collingwood and her two daughters, who were great authorities upon the question, and held a Dorcas society once a week, of which Milly and I were members.

There was the usual music—a little playing and a little singing from the younger ladies of the company, myself included. Milly sang an English ballad very sweetly, and Angus Egerton stood by the piano looking down at her while she sang.

Did he fall in love with her upon this first happy evening that those two spent together? I cannot tell; but it
is certain that after that evening, he seemed to haunt us
in our walks, and, go where we would, we were always
meeting him, in company with a Scottish deerhound
called Nestor, of which Milly became very fond. When
we met in this half-accidental way he used to join us in
our walk for a mile or two, very often bearing us company till we were within a few paces of Thornleigh.

These meetings, utterly accidental as they always were
on our side, were a source of some perplexity to me. I
was not quite certain whether I was right in sanction-
ing so close an acquaintance between Emily Darrell
and the master of Cumber Priory. I knew that her father thought badly of him. Yet, what could I do? I was
not old enough to pretend to any authority over my
darling, nor had her father invested me with any; and
I knew that her noble nature was worthy of all confidence. Beyond this, I liked Angus Egerton, and was
inclined to trust him. So the time slipped away very
pleasantly for all of us, and the friendship among us all
three became closer day by day.

We met Mr. Egerton very often at the Rectory, and sometimes at other houses where we visited. He was much
liked by the Thornleigh people, who had, most of them,
known him in his boyhood; and it was considered by
his old friends, that, whatever his career abroad might
have been, he had begun, and was steadily pursuing, a
reformed course of life. His means did not enable him
to do much, but he was doing a little towards the improvement of Cumber Priory; and his existence there
was as simple as that of the Master of Ravenswood.

I had noticed that Mrs. Collingwood did all in her power to encourage the friendship between Milly and Mr.

Egerton, and one day in the spring, after they had met a great many times at her house, she spoke to me of her hopes quite openly.

It was a bright afternoon, and we were all strolling in the garden, after a game of croquet—the Rector's wife and I side by side, Milly and Angus a little way in front of us.

'I think she likes him,' Mrs. Collingwood said thoughtfully.

'Everybody seems to like Mr. Egerton,' I answered.

'O yes, I know that; but I mean something more than the ordinary liking. I am so anxious that he should marry—and marry wisely. I think I am almost as fond of him as if he were my son; and I should be so pleased if I could be the means of bringing about a match between them. Milly is just the girl to make a man happy, and her fortune would restore Cumber Priory to all its old glory.'

Her fortune! The word jarred upon me. Was it her money, after all, that Angus Egerton was thinking of when he took such pains to pursue my darling?

'I should be sorry for her to marry any one who cared for her money,' I said.

'Of course, my dear Miss Crofton; and so should I be sorry to see her throw herself away upon any one with whom her money was a paramount consideration. But one cannot put these things quite out of the question. I know that Angus admired her very much the first day he saw her, and I fancy his admiration has grown into a warmer feeling since then. He has said nothing to me upon the subject, nor I to him; for you know how silent he always is about himself. But I cannot help wishing that such a thing might come to pass. He has one of the best names in the North Riding, and a first-rate position as the owner of Cumber Priory. He only wants money.'

I was too young and inexperienced to take a worldly view of things, and from this moment felt disposed to distrust Mr. Egerton. I remembered the story of his early attachment, and told myself that a man who had loved once like that had in all probability worn out his powers of loving.

'I don't think Mr. Darrell would approve of, or even permit, such a marriage,' I said presently. 'I know he has a very bad opinion of Mr. Egerton.'

'On what account?'

'On account of his conduct to his mother.'

'No one knows the secret of that affair except Angus himself,' answered Mrs. Collingwood. 'I don't think any one has a right to think badly of him upon that ground. I knew Mrs. Egerton very well. She was a proud hard woman, capable of almost anything in order to accomplish any set purpose of her own. Up to the time when he went to Oxford Angus had been an excellent son.'

'Was it at Oxford he met the girl he wanted to marry?'

'No; it was somewhere in the west of England, where he went on a walking tour during the long vacation.'

'He must have loved her very much, to act as he did. I should doubt his power ever to love any one else.'

'That is quite a girl's way of thinking, my dear Miss Crofton. Depend upon it, after that kind of stormy first love, there generally comes a better and truer feeling. Angus was little more than a boy then. He is in the prime of manhood now, able to judge wisely, and not easily to be caught, or he would have married in all those years abroad.'

This seemed reasonable enough; but I was vexed, nevertheless, by Mrs. Collingwood's match-making notions, which seemed to disturb the peaceful progress of our lives. After this I looked upon every invitation to the Rectory—where we never went without meeting Mr. Egerton—as a kind of snare; but our visits there were always very pleasant, and I grew in time to think with more indulgence of the Rector's wife's desire for her favourite's advantage.

In all this time Angus Egerton had in no manner betrayed the state of his feelings. If he met us in our walks oftener than seemed possible by mere chance, there was nothing strictly lover-like in his tone or conduct. But I have seen his face light up as he met my dear girl at these times, and I have noticed a certain softening of his voice as he talked to her, that I never heard on other occasions.

And she? About her feelings I had much less doubt. She tried her uttermost to hide the truth from me, ashamed of her regard for one who had never yet professed to be more than a friend; but I knew that she loved him. It was impossible, in the perfect companionship and confidence of our lives, for Milly to keep this first secret of her pure young heart hidden from me. I knew that she loved him; and I began to look forward anxiously to Mr. Darrell's return, which would relieve me of all responsibility, and perhaps put an end to our friendship with Angus Egerton.

CHAPTER VIII

On the Watch

The travellers came back to Thornleigh Manor in August, when the days were breathless and sultry, and the freshness of the foliage had already begun to fade after an unusually dry summer. Milly and I had been very happy together, and I think we both looked forward with a vague dread to the coming break in our lives. She loved her father as dearly as she had ever done, and longed ardently to see him again; but she knew as well as I did that our independence must end with his return.

'If he were coming back alone, Mary,' she said—'if that marriage were all a dream, and he were coming back alone—how happy I should be! I know that of is own free will he would never come between me and any wish of mine. But I don't know how he would act under his wife's influence. You cannot imagine the power she has over him. And we shall have to begin the old false life over again, she and I— disliking and distrusting each other in our hearts—the daily round of civilities and ceremonies and pretences. O Mary, you cannot think how I hate it.'

We had seen nothing of Julian Stormont during all the time of our happy solitude; but on the day appointed for Mr. and Mrs. Darrell's return he came to Thornleigh, looking more careworn than ever. I pitied him a little, knowing the state of his feelings about Milly, believing indeed that he loved her with a rare intensity, and being inclined to attribute the change in him to his disappointment upon this subject.

Milly told him how ill he was looking, and he said something about hard work and late hours, with a little bitter laugh.

'It doesn't matter to any one whether I am well or ill, you see, Milly,' he said. 'What would any one care if I were to drop over the side of the quay some dark night, on my way from the office to my lodgings, after a hard day's work, and never be seen alive again?'

'How wicked it is of you to talk like that, Julian! There are plenty of people who would care—papa, to begin with.'

'Well, I suppose my uncle William would be rather sorry. He would lose a good man of business, and he would scarcely like going back to the counting-house, and giving himself up to all the dry details of commerce once more.'

The travellers arrived soon after this. Mr. Darrell greeted his daughter with much tenderness; but I noticed a kind of languor in Mrs. Darrell's embrace, very different from her reception of Milly at that first meeting which I had witnessed more than a year before. It seemed to me that her power over her husband was now supreme, and that she did not trouble herself to keep up any pretence of affection for his only child.

She was dressed to perfection; and that subdued charm which was scarcely beauty, and yet stood in place of it, attracted me to-day as it had done when we first met. She was a woman who, I could imagine, might be more admired than many handsomer women. There was a distinction, an originality about the pale delicate face, dark arched brows, and gray eyes—eyes which were at times very brilliant.

She looked round her without the faintest show of interest or admiration as she loitered with her husband on the terrace, while innumerable travelling-bags, shawls, books, newspapers, and packages were being carried from the barouche to the house.

'How dry and burnt-up everything looks!' she said.

'Have you no better greeting than that for Thornleigh, my dear Augusta?' Mr. Darrell asked in rather a wounded tone. 'I thought you would be pleased to see the old place again.'

'Thornleigh Manor is not a passion of mine,' she answered. 'I hope you will take a house in town at the beginning of next year.'

She passed on into the hall, after having honoured me with the coldest possible shake-hands. We saw no more of her until nearly dinner-time, when she came down to the drawing-room, dressed in white, and looking deliciously pale and cool in the sultry weather. Milly had spent the afternoon in going round the gardens and home-farm with her father, and had thoroughly enjoyed the delight of a couple of hours alone with him. She gave him up now to Mrs. Darrell, who devoted all her attention to him for the rest of the evening; while Julian Stormont, Milly, and I loitered about the garden, and played a desultory game of croquet.

It was not until the next morning that Mr. Egerton's name was mentioned, although it had been in my thoughts, and I cannot doubt in Milly's, ever since Mr. Darrell's arrival. We were in the drawing-room after breakfast, not quite decided what to do with the day, when Mr. Darrell came into the room dressed for a ride with his wife. He went over to the window by which Milly was standing.

'You have quite given up riding, Ellis tells me, my dear,' he said.

'I have not cared to ride while you were away, papa, as Mary does not ride.'

'Miss Crofton might have learnt to ride; there would always be a horse at her disposal.'

'We like walking better,' Milly said, blushing a little, and fidgeting nervously with one of the buttons on her father's coat. 'I used to feel in the way, you know, when I rode with you and Mrs. Darrell.'

'That was your own fault, Milly,' he answered, with a displeased look.

'I suppose it was. But I think Augusta felt it too. O, by the bye, papa, I did not tell you quite all the news when we were out together yesterday.'

'Indeed!'

'No; I forgot to mention that Mr. Egerton has come back.'

'Angus Egerton?'

'Yes; he came back last winter.'

'You never said so in your letters.'

'Didn't I? I suppose that was because I knew you were rather prejudiced against him; and one can't explain away that kind of thing in a letter.'

'You would find it very difficult to explain away my dislike of Angus Egerton, either in or out of a letter. Have you seen much of him?'

'A good deal. He has been at the Rectory very often when Mary and I have been invited there. The Collingwoods are very fond of him. I am sure—I think—you will like him, papa, when you come to see a little of him. He is going to call upon you.'

'He can come if he pleases,' Mr. Darrell answered with an indifferent air; 'I shall not be uncivil to him. But I am rather sorry that he has made such a favourable impression upon you, Milly.'

She was still playing with the buttons of his coat, looking downward, her dark eyes quite veiled by their long lashes.

'I did not say that, papa,' she murmured shyly.

'But I am sure of it from your manner. Has he done anything towards the improvement of Cumber?'

'O yes; he has put new roofs to some part of the stables; and the land is in better order, they say; and the gardens are kept nicely now.'

'Does he live alone at the Priory?'

'Quite alone, papa.'

'He must find it rather a dull business, I should think.'

'Mr. Collingwood says he is very fond of study, and that he has a wonderful collection of old books. He is a great smoker too, I believe; he walks a good deal; and he hunted all last winter. They say he is a tremendous rider.'

Augusta Darrell came in at this moment, ready for her ride. Her slim willowy figure looked to great advantage in the plain tight-fitting cloth habit; and the little felt hat with its bright scarlet feather gave a coquettish expression to her face. She tapped her husband lightly on the arm with her riding-whip.

'Now, William, if your are quite ready.'

'My dearest, I have been waiting for the last half-hour.'

They went off to their horses. Milly followed them to the terrace, and watched them as they rode away.

We spent the morning out-of-doors sketching, with Julian Stormont in attendance upon us. At two o'clock we all meet at luncheon.

After luncheon Milly and I went to the drawing-room, while Mrs. Darrell and Mr. Stormont strolled upon the terrace. My dear girl had a sort of restless manner to-day, and went from one occupation to another, now sitting for a few minutes at the piano, playing brief snatches of pensive melody, now taking up a book, only to throw it down again with a little weary sigh. She seated herself at a table presently, and began to arrange the sketches in her portfolio. While she was doing this a servant announced Mr. Egerton. She rose hurriedly, blushing as I had rarely seen her blush before, and looking towards the open window near her, almost as if she would have liked to make her escape from the room. It was the first time Angus Egerton had been at Thornleigh Manor since she was a little child.

'Tell papa that Mr. Egerton is here, Filby,' she said to the servant. 'I think you will find him in the library.'

She had recovered her self-possession in some measure by the time she came forward to shake hands with the visitor; and in a few minutes we were talking in the usual easy friendly way.

'You see, I have lost no time in calling upon your papa, Miss Darrell,' he said presently. 'I am not too proud to show him how anxious I am to regain his friendship, if, indeed, I ever possessed it.'

Mr. Darrell came into the room as he was speaking; and however coldly he might have intended to receive the master of Cumber Priory, his manner soon softened and grew more cordial. There was a certain kind of charm about Angus Egerton, not very easily to be described, which I think had a potent influence upon all who knew him.

I fancied that Mr. Darrell felt this, and struggled against it, and ended by giving way to it. I saw that he watched his daughter closely, even anxiously, when she was talking to Angus Egerton, as if he had already some suspicion about the state of her feelings with regard to him. Mr. Egerton had caught sight of the open portfolio, and had insisted on looking over the sketches—not the first of Milly's that he had seen by a great many. I noticed the grave, almost tender, smile with which he looked at the little artistic 'bits' out of Cumber Wood. He went on talking to Mr. Darrell all the time he was looking at these sketches; talking of the neighbourhood and the changes that had come about of late years, and a little of the Priory, and his intentions with regard to improvements.

'I can only creep along at a snail's pace,' he said; 'for I am determined not to get into debt, and I won't sell.'

'I wonder you never tried to let the priory in all those years that you were abroad,' suggested Mr. Darrell.

Mr. Egerton shook his head, with a smile.

'I couldn't bring myself to that,' he said, 'though I wanted money badly enough. There has never been a strange master at Cumber since it belonged to the Egertons. I daresay it's a foolish piece of sentimentality on my part; but I had rather fancy the old place rotting slowly to decay than in the occupation of strangers.'

He was standing by the table where the open portfolio lay, with Milly by his side, and one of the sketches in his hands, when Mrs. Darrell came in at the window nearest to this little group, and stood on the threshold looking at him. I think I was the only person who saw her face at that moment. It was so sudden a look that came upon it, a look half terror, half pain, and it passed away so quickly, that I had scarcely time to distinguish the expression before it was gone; but it was a look that brought back to my memory the almost forgotten scene in the little study at Cumber Priory, and set me wondering what it could be that made the sight of Angus Egerton, either on canvas or in the flesh, a cause of agitation to Milly's stepmother.

In the next moment Mr. Darrell was presenting his visitor to his wife; and as the two acknowledged the introduction, I stole a glance at Mr. Egerton's face. It was paler than usual; and the expression of Mrs. Darrell's countenance seemed in a manner reflected in it. It was not possible that such looks could be without some significance. I felt convinced that these two people had met before.

There was a change in Mr. Egerton's manner from the moment of that introduction. He laid down Milly's sketch without another word, and stood with his eyes fixed on Augusta Darrell's face with a strange half-bewildered look, like a man who doubts the evidence of his own senses. Mrs. Darrell, on the contrary, seemed, after that one look which I had seen, quite at her ease, and rattled on gaily about the delight of travelling in the Tyrol, as compared to the dulness of life at Thornleigh.

'I hope you will enliven us a little, Mr. Egerton,' she said. 'It is quite an agreeable surprise to find a new neighbour.'

'I ought to be very much flattered by that remark; but I doubt my power to add to the liveliness of this part of the world. And I do not think I shall stay much longer at Cumber.'

Milly glanced up at him with a surprised look.

'Mrs. Collingwood told us you were quite settled at the Priory,' she said, 'and that you intended to spend the rest of your days as a country squire.'

'I may have dreamed such a dream sometimes, Miss Darrell; but there are dreams that never fulfil themselves.'

He had recovered himself by this time, and spoke in his accustomed tone. Mr. Darrell asked him to dinner on an early day, when I knew the Rectory people were coming to us, and the invitation was accepted.

Julian Stormont had followed Mrs. Darrell in from the terrace, and had remained in the background, a very attentive listener and observer during the conversation that followed.

'So that is Angus Egerton,' he said, when our visitor had left us.

'Yes, Julian. O, by the bye, I forgot to introduce you; you came in so quietly,' answered Mr. Darrell.

'I can't say I particularly care about the honour of knowing that gentleman,' said Mr. Stormont in a half-contemptuous tone.

'Why not?' Milly asked quickly.

'Because I never heard any goof of him.'

'But he has reformed, it seems,' said Mr. Darrell, 'and is leading quite a steady life at Cumber, the Collingwoods tell me. Augusta and I called at the Rectory this morning, and the Rector and his wife talked a good deal of him. I was rather pleased with him, I confess, just now.'

Milly looked up at her father gratefully. Poor child! how innocently and unconsciously she betrayed her secret! and how little she thought of the jealous eyes that were watching her! I saw Julian Stormont's face darken with an angry look, and I knew that he had already discovered the state of Milly's feelings in relation to Angus Egerton.

He was still with us when Mr. Egerton came to dinner two days later. I shall never forget that evening. The day was oppressively warm, with that dry sultry heat of which there had been so much during the latter part of the summer; and as the afternoon advanced, the air grew still, that palpable stillness which so often comes before a thunder-storm. Milly had been full of life and vivacity all day, flitting from room to room with a kind of joyous restlessness. She took unusual pains with her toilette for so simple a party, and came into my room looking like Titania in her gauzy white dress, with half-blown blush-roses in her hair, and more roses in a bouquet at her waist.

Mr. Egerton came in a little later than the party from the Rectory, and after shaking hands with Mr. Darrell, made his way at once to the place where Milly and I were sitting.

'Any more sketching since I was here last, Miss Darrell?' he asked.

'No. I have been doing nothing for the last day or two.'

'Do you know I have been thinking of your work in that way a good deal since I called here. I am stronger in criticism than in execution, you know. I think I was giving you a little lecture on your shortcomings, wasn't I?'

'Yes; but you left off so abruptly in the middle of it, that I don't fancy it was very profitable to me,' Milly answered in rather a piqued tone.

'Did I really? O yes, I remember. I was quite startled by Mrs. Darrell's appearance. She is so surprisingly like a lady I knew a long time ago.'

'That is rather a curious coincidence,' I said.

'How a coincidence?' asked Mr. Egerton.

'Mrs. Darrell said almost the same thing about your portrait when we were at Cumber one day. It reminded her of some one she had known long ago.'

'What an excellent memory you have for small events, Miss Crofton!' said a voice close behind me.

It was Mrs. Darrell's. She had come across the room towards us, unobserved by me, at any rate. Whether Angus Egerton had seen her or not, I do not know. He rose to shake hands with her, and then went on talking about Milly's sketching.

Mr. Collingwood took Mrs. Darrell in to dinner, and Mr. Egerton gave his arm to Milly, and was seated next her at the prettily decorated table, upon which there was always a wealth of roses at this time of year. I saw Augusta Darrell's eye wander restlessly in that direction many times during dinner, and I felt that the dear girl I loved so fondly was in an atmosphere of falsehood. What was the nature of the past acquaintance between those two people? and why was it tacitly denied by both of them? If it had been an ordinary friendship, there could have been no reason for this concealment and suppression. I had never quite made up my mind to trust Angus Egerton, though I liked and admired him; and this mysterious relation between him and Augusta Darrell was a sufficient cause for serious distrust.

'I wish she cared for him less,' I said to myself, as I glanced at Milly's bright happy face.

When we went back to the drawing-room after dinner, the Miss Collingwoods had a great deal to say to Milly about a grand croquet-match which was to take place in a week or two at Pensildon, Sir john and Lady Pensildon's place, fourteen miles from Thornleigh. The Rector's daughters, both of whom were several years older than Milly, were passionately fond of croquet and everything in the way of gaiety, and were full of excitement about this coming event, discussing what they were going to wear, and what Milly was going to wear, on the occasion. While they were engaged in this way, Mrs. Collingwood told me a long story about one of her poor parishioners, always an inexhaustible subject with her. This arrangement left Mrs. Darrell unoccupied; and after standing at one of the open windows looking listlessly out, she sauntered out upon the terrace, her favourite lounge always in this summer weather. I saw her repass the windows a few minutes afterwards, in earnest conversation with Angus Egerton. This was some time before the other gentlemen left the dining-room; and they were still walking slowly up and down when Mr. Darrell and the Rector came to the drawing-room. The storm had not yet come, and it was bright moonlight. Mr. Darrell went out and brought his wife in, with some gentle reproof on her imprudence in re-maining out of doors so late in her thin muslin dress.

After this there came some music. Augusta Darrell sang some old English ballads which I had never heard her sing before—simple pathetic melodies, which, I think, brought tears to the eyes of all of us.

Mr. Egerton sat near one of the open windows, with his face in shadow, while she was singing; and as she began the last of these old songs he rose with a half-impatient gesture, and went out upon the terrace. If I watched him closely, and others in relation to him, at this time, it was from no frivolous or impertinent curiosity, but because I felt very certain that my darling's happiness was at stake. I saw her little disappointed look when he remained at the farther end of the room, talking to the gentlemen, all the rest of that evening, instead of con-triving by some means to be near her, as he always had done during our pleasant evenings at the Rectory.

CHAPTER IX

Angus Egerton is Rejected

The expected storm came next day, and Milly and I were caught in it. We had gone for a ramble across the moor, and were luckily within a short distance of Rebecca Thatcher's cottage when the first vivid flash broke through the leaden clouds, and the first long peal of thunder came crashing over the open landscape. We set off for Mrs. Thatcher's habitation at a run, and arrived there breathless.

The herbalist was not alone. A tall dark figure stood between us and the little window as we went in, blotting out all the light.

Milly gave a faint cry of surprise; and as the figure turned towards us I recognised Mr. Egerton.

In all our visits among the poor we had never met him before.

'Caught again, young ladies!' he cried, laughing; 'you've neither of you grown weatherwise yet, I see. Luckily you're under cover before the rain has begun. I think we shall have it pretty heavy presently. How surprised you look to see me here, Miss Darrell! Becky is a very old friend of mine. I remember her ever since I can remember anything. She was in my grandfather's service once upon a time.'

'That I was, Mr. Egerton, and there's nothing I wouldn't do for you and yours—for you at least, for there's none but you left now. But I suppose you'll be getting married one of these days; you're not going to let the old name of Egerton die out?'

Angus Egerton shook his head with a slow sad gesture.

'I am too poor to marry, Mrs. Thatcher,' he said. 'What could I offer a wife but a gloomy old house, and a perpetual struggle to make hundreds do the work of thousands? I am too proud to ask the woman I love to sacrifice her future to me.'

'Cumber Priory is good enough for any woman that ever lived,' answered Rebecca Thatcher. 'You don't mean what you say, Mr. Egerton. You know that the name you bear is counted better than money in these parts.'

He laughed, and changed the conversation.

'I heard you young ladies talking a great deal of the Pensildon fete last night,' he said.

'Did you really?' asked Milly; 'you did not appear to be much interested in our conversation.'

'Did I seem distrait? It is a way I have sometimes, Miss Darrell; but I can assure you I can hear two or three conversations at once. I think I heard all that you and the Miss Collingwoods were saying.'

'You are going to Lady Pensildon's on the 31st, I suppose?' Milly said.

'I think not. I think of going abroad for the autumn. I have been rather a long time at Cumber, you know, and I'm afraid the roving mood is coming upon me again. I shall be sorry to go, too, for I had intended to torment you continually about your art studies. You have really a genius for landscape, you know, Miss Darrell; you only want to be goaded into industry now and then by some severe critic like myself. Is your cousin, Mr. Stormont, an artist, by the way?'

'Not at all.'

'That's a pity. He seems a clever young man. I suppose he will be a good deal with you, now that Mr. and Mrs. Darrell have returned?'

'He cannot stay very long at a time. He has the chief position in papa's counting-house.'

'Indeed! He looked a little as if the cares of business weighed upon his spirit.'

He glanced rather curiously at Milly while he was speaking of Mr. Stormont. Was he really going away, I wondered, or was that threat of departure only a lover-like ruse?

The rain came presently with all the violence usual to a thunder-shower. We were prisoners in Mrs. Thatcher's cottage for more than an hour; a happy hour, I think, to Milly, in spite of the closeness of the atmosphere and the medical odour of the herbs. Angus Egerton stood beside her chair all the time, looking down at her bright face and talking to her; while Mrs. Thatcher mumbled a long catalogue of her ailments and troubles into my somewhat inattentive ear.

Once while those two were talking about his intended departure I heard Mr. Egerton say,

'If I thought any one cared about my staying—if I could believe that any one would miss me ever so little—I should be in no hurry to leave Yorkshire.'

Of course Milly told him that there were many people who would miss him—Mr. Collingwood for instance, and all the family at the Rectory. He bent over her, and said something in a very low voice—something that brought vivid blushes to her face; and a few minutes afterwards they went to the door to look at the weather, and stood there talking till I have heard the last of Mrs. Thatcher's woes, and was free to join them. I had never seen Milly look so lovely as she did just then, with her downcast eyes, and a little tremulous smile upon her perfect mouth.

Mr. Egerton walked all the way home with us. The storm was quite over, the sun shining, and the air full of that cool freshness which comes after rain. We talked of all kinds of things. Mr. Egerton had almost made up his mind to spend the autumn at Cumber, he told us; and he would go to the Pensildon fete, and take Milly's side in the croquet-match. He seemed in almost boyish spirits during that homeward walk.

When we went up-stairs to our rooms that night, Milly followed me into mine. There was nothing new in this; we often wasted half an hour in happy idle talk before going to bed; but I was sure from my darling's manner she had something to tell me. She went over to an open window, and stood there with her face turned away from me, looking out across the distant moonlit sea.

'Mary,' she said, after a very long pause, 'do you think people are intended to be quite happy in this world?'

'My dear love, how can I answer such a question as that? I think that many people have their lives in their own hands, and that it rests with themselves to find happiness. And there are many natures that are elevated and purified by sorrow. I cannot tell what is best for us, dear. I cannot pretend to guess what this life was meant to be.'

'There is something in perfect happiness that frightens one, Mary. It seems as if it could not last. If it could, if I dared believe in it, I should think that my life was going to be quite happy.'

'Why should it be otherwise, my dear Milly? I don't think you have ever known much sorrow.'

'Not since my mother died—and I was only a child then—but that old pain has never quite gone out of my heart; and papa's marriage has been a greater grief to me than you would believe, Mary. This house has never seemed to be really my home since then. No, dear, it is a new life that is dawning for me—and O, such a bright one!'

She put her arms round my neck, and hid her face upon my shoulder.

'Can you guess what Angus Egerton said to me to-day?' she asked, in a low tremulous voice.

'Was it something very wonderful, dear—or something as old as the world we live in?'

'Not old to me, Mary—new and wonderful beyond all measure. I did not think he cared for me—I had never dared to hope; for I have liked him a little for a long time, dear, though I don't suppose you ever thought so.'

'My dear girl, I have known it from the very beginning. There is nothing in the world more transparent than your thoughts about Angus Egerton have been to me.'

'O Mary, how could you! And I have been so careful to say nothing!' she cried reproachfully. 'But he loves me, dear. He has loved me for a long time, he says; and he has asked me to be his wife.'

'What, after all those protestations about never asking a woman to share his poverty?'

'Yes, Mary; and he meant what he said. He told me that if I had been a penniless girl, he should have proposed to me ever so long ago. And he is to see papa to-morrow.'

'Do you think Mr. Darrell will ever consent to such a marriage, Milly?' I asked gravely.

'Why should he not? He cannot go on thinking badly of Angus when every one else thinks so well of him. You must have seen how he has softened towards him since they met. Mr. Egerton's old family and position are quite an equivalent for my money, whatever that may be. O Mary, I don't think papa can refuse his consent.'

'I am rather doubtful about that, Milly. It's one thing to like Mr. Egerton very well as a visitor—quite another to accept him as a son-in-law. Frankly, my dearest, I fear your father will be against the match.'

'Mary,' cried Milly reproachfully, 'I can see what it is— you are prejudiced against Mr. Egerton.'

'I am only anxious for your welfare, darling. I like Mr. Egerton very much. It is difficult for any one to avoid liking him. But I confess that I cannot bring myself to put entire trust in him.'

'Why not?'

I did not like to tell her the chief reason for my distrust— that mysterious relation between Angus Egerton and

Mrs. Darrell. The subject was a serious—almost a dangerous—one; and I had no positive evidence to bring forward in proof of my fancy. It was a question of looks and words that had been full of significance to me, but which might seem to Milly to mean very little.

'We cannot help our instinctive doubts, dear. But if you can trust Mr. Egerton, and if your father can trust him, my fancies can matter very little. I cannot stand between you and your love, dear—I know that.'

'But you can make me very unhappy by your doubts, Mary,' she answered.

I kissed her, and did my best to console her; but she was not easily to be comforted, and left me in a half-sorrowful, half-angry mood. I had disappointed her, she told me—she had felt so sure of my sympathy; and instead of sharing her happiness, I had made her miserable by my fanciful doubts and gloomy forebodings. After she had gone, I sat by the window for a long time, thinking of her disconsolately, and feeling myself very guilty. But I had a fixed conviction that Mr. Darrell would refuse to receive Angus Egerton as his daughter's suitor, and that the course of this love-affair was not destined to be a smooth one.

The result proved that I had been right. Mr. Egerton had a long interview with Mr. Darrell in the library next morning, during which his proposal was most firmly rejected. Milly and I knew that he was in the house, and my poor girl walked up and down our sitting-room with nervously clasped hands and an ashy pale face all the time those two were together down-stairs.

She turned to me with a little piteous look when she heard Angus Egerton ride away from the front of the house.

'O Mary, what is my fate to be?' she asked. 'I think he has been rejected. I do not think he would have gone away without seeing me if the interview had ended happily.'

A servant came to summon us both to the library. We went down together, Milly's cold hand clasped in mine.

Mr. Darrell was not alone. His wife was sitting with her back to the window, very pale, and with an angry brightness in her eyes.

'Sit down, Miss Crofton,' Mr. Darrell said very coldly; 'and you, Milly, come here.'

She went towards him with a slow faltering step, and sank down into the chair to which he pointed, looking at him all the time in an eager beseeching way that I think must have gone to his heart. He was standing with his back to the empty fireplace, and remained standing throughout the interview.

'I think you know that I love you, Milly,' he began, 'and that your happiness is the chief desire of my mind.'

'I'm sure of that, papa.'

'And yet you have deceived me.'

'Deceived you? O papa, in what way?'

'By encouraging the hopes of a man whom you must have known I would never receive as your husband; by suffering your feelings to become engaged, without one word of warning to me, and in a manner that you must have known could not fail to be most obnoxious to me.'

'O papa, I did not know; it was only yesterday that Mr. Egerton spoke for the first time. There has been nothing hidden from you.'

'Nothing? Do you call your intimate acquaintance with this man nothing? He may have delayed any actual declaration until my return— with an artful appearance of consideration for me; but some kind of love-affair must have been going on between you all the time.'

'No, indeed, papa; until yesterday there was never anything but the most ordinary acquaintance. Mary knows—'

'Pray don't appeal to Miss Crofton,' her father interrupted sternly. 'Miss Crofton has done very wrong in encouraging this affair. Miss Crofton heard my opinion of Angus Egerton a long time ago.'

'Mary has done nothing to encourage our acquaintance. It has been altogether a matter of accident from first to last. What have you said to Mr. Egerton, papa? Tell me at once, please.'

She said this with a quiet firmness, looking bravely up at him all the while.

'I have told him that nothing would induce me to consent to such a marriage. I have forbidden him ever to see you again.'

'That seems very hard, papa.'

'I thought you knew my opinion of Mr. Egerton.'

'It would change if you knew more of him.'

'Never. I might like him very well as a member of society; I could never approve of him as a son-in-law. Besides, I have other views for you—long-cherished views—which I hope you will not disappoint.'

'I don't know what you mean by that, papa; but I know that I can never marry any one except Mr. Egerton. I may never marry at all, if you refuse to change your decision upon this subject; but I am quite sure I shall never be the wife of any one else.'

Her father looked at her angrily. That hard expression about the lower part of the face, which I had noticed in his portrait and in himself from the very first, was intensified to-day. He looked a stern resolute man, whose will was not to be moved by a daughter's pleading.

'We shall see about that by and by,' he said. 'I am not going to have my plans defeated by a girl's folly. I have been a very indulgent father, but I am not a weak or yielding one. You will have to obey me, Milly, or you will find yourself a substantial sufferer by and by.'

'If you mean that you will disinherit me, papa, I am quite willing that you should do that,' Milly answered resolutely. 'Perhaps you think Mr. Egerton cares for my fortune. Put him to the test, papa. Tell him that you will give me nothing, and that be may take me on that condition.'

Augusta Darrell turned upon her stepdaughter with a sudden look in her face that was almost like a flame.

'Do you think him so disinterested?' she asked. 'Have you such supreme confidence in his affection?'

'Perfect confidence.'

'And you do not believe that mercenary considerations have any weight with him? You do not think that he is eager to repair his shattered fortunes? You think him all truth and devotion? He, a *blase* man of the world, of three-and-thirty; a man who has outlived the possibility of anything like a real attachment; a man who lavished his whole stock of feeling upon the one attachment of his youth.'

She said all this very quietly, but with a suppressed bitterness. I think it needed all her powers of restraint to keep her from some passionate outburst that would have betrayed the secret of her life. I was now more than ever convinced that she had known Angus Egerton in the past, and that she had loved him.

'You see, I am not afraid of his being put to the test,' Milly said proudly. 'I know he loved some one very dearly, a long time ago. He spoke of that yesterday. He told me that his old love had died out of his heart years ago.'

'He told you a lie,' cried Mrs. Darrell. 'Such things never die. They sleep, perhaps—like the creatures that hide themselves in the ground and lie torpid all the winter—but with one breath of the past they flame into life again.'

'I am not going to make any such foolish trial of your lover's faith, Milly,' said Mr. Darrell. 'Whether your fortune is or is not a paramount consideration with him can make no possible difference in my decision. Nothing will ever induce me to consent to your marrying him. Of course, if you choose to defy me, you are of age and your own mistress; but on the day that makes you Angus Egerton's wife you will cease to be my daughter.'

'Papa,' cried Milly, 'you will break my heart.'

'Nonsense, child; hearts are not easily broken. Let me hear no more of this unfortunate business. I have spoken to you very plainly, in order that there might be no chance of misunderstanding between us; and I rely upon your honour that there shall be no clandestine meeting between you and Angus Egerton in the future. I look to you, Miss Crofton, also, and shall hold you answerable for any accidental encounters out walking.'

'You need not be afraid, papa,' Milly answered disconsolately. 'I daresay Mr. Egerton will leave Yorkshire, as he spoke of doing yesterday.'

'I hope he may,' said Mr. Darrell.

Milly rose to leave the room. Half-way towards the door she stopped, and turned her white despairing face towards her father with a hopeless look.

'I shall obey you, papa,' she said. 'I could not bear to forfeit your love, even for his sake. But I think you will break my heart.'

Mr. Darrell went over to her and kissed her.

'I am acting best for your ultimate happiness, Milly, be sure of that,' he said in a kinder tone than he had used before. 'There, my love, go and be happy with Miss Crofton, and let us all agree to forget this business as quickly as possible.'

This was our dismissal. We went back to Milly's pretty sitting-room, where the sun was shining and the warm summer air blowing on birds and flowers, and books and drawing materials, and all the airy trifles that had made our lives pleasant to us until that hour. Milly sat on a low stool at my feet, and buried her face in my lap, refusing all comfort. She sat like this for about an hour, weeping silently, and then rose suddenly and wiped the tears from her pale face.

'I am not going to lead you a miserable life about this, Mary,' she said. 'We will never speak of it after to-day. And I will try to do my duty to papa, and bear my life without that new happiness, which made it seem so bright. Do you think Mr. Egerton will feel the disappointment very much, Mary?'

'He cannot help feeling it, dear, if he loves you—as I believe he does.'

'And we might have been so happy together! I was dreaming of Cumber Priory all last night. I thought it had been restored with some of my money, and that the old house was full of life and brightness. Will he go away, do you think, Mary?'

'I should think it very likely.'

'And I shall never see him any more. I could not forfeit papa's love, Mary.'

'It would be a hard thing if you were to do that for the sake of a stranger, dear.'

'No, no, Mary; he is not a stranger to me; Angus Egerton is not a stranger. I know that he is noble and good. But my father was all the world to me a year ago. I could not do without his love. I must obey him.'

'Believe me, dear, it will be wisest and best to do so. You cannot tell what changes may come to pass in the future. Obedience will make you very dear to your father; and the time may come in which he will think better of Mr. Egerton.'

'O Mary, if I could hope that!'

'Hope for everything, dear, if you do your duty.'

She grew a little more cheerful after this, and met her father at diner with quite a placid face, though it was still very pale. Mrs. Darrell looked at her wonderingly, and with a half-contemptuous expression, I thought, as if this passion of her step-daughter's seemed to her a very poor thing, after all.

Before the week was out, we heard that Mr. Egerton had left Yorkshire. We did not go to the Pensildon fete. Milly had a cold and kept her room, much to the regret of the Miss Collingwoods, who called every day to inquire about her. She made this cold—which was really a very slight affair—an excuse for a week's solitude, and at the end of that time reappeared among us with no trace of her secret sorrow. It was only I, who was always with her, and knew her to the core of her heart, who could have told how hard a blow that disappointment had been, and how much it cost her to bear it so quietly.

CHAPTER X

Changes at Thornleigh

The autumn and the early winter passed monoto-
nously enough. There was a good deal of company
at Thornleigh Manor at first, for Mrs. Darrell hated solitude; but after a little time she grew tired of the people
her husband knew, and the dinners and garden parties
became less frequent. I had found out, very soon after her return, that she was not happy—that this easy
prosperous life was in some manner a burden to her. It
was only in her husband's presence that she made any
pretence of being pleased or interested in things. With
him she was always the same—always deferential, af-
fectionate, and attentive; while he, on his side, was the
devoted slave of her every whim and wish.

She was not unkind to Milly, but those two seemed in-
stinctively to avoid each other.

The winter brought trouble to Thornleigh Manor. It was
well for Milly that she had tried to do her duty to her
father, and had submitted herself patiently to his will.
About a fortnight before Christmas Mr. Darrell went to
North Shields to make his annual investigation of the
wharves and warehouses, and to take a kind of review

of the year's business. He never returned alive. He was seized with an apoplectic fit in the office, and carried to his hotel speechless. His wife and Milly were summoned by a telegraphic message, and started for Shields by the first train that could convey them there; but they were too late. He expired an hour before their arrival.

I need not dwell upon the details of that sad time. Milly felt the blow severely; and it was long before I saw her smile, after that dark December day on which the fatal summons came. She had lost much of her joyousness and brightness after the disappointment about Angus Egerton, and this new sorrow quite crushed her.

They brought Mr. Darrell's remains to Thornleigh, and he was buried in the family vault under the noble old church, where his father and mother, his first wife, and a son who died in infancy had been buried before him. He had been very popular in the neighbourhood, and was sincerely regretted by all who had known him.

Julius Stormont was chief-mourner at the unpretentious funeral. He seemed much affected by his uncle's death; and his manner towards his cousin had an unusual gentleness.

I was present at the reading of the will, which took place in the dining-room immediately after the funeral. Mrs. Darrell, Milly, Mr. Stormont, myself, and the family lawyer were the only persons assembled in the spacious room, which had a dreary look without the chief of the household.

The will had been made a few months after Mr. Darrell's second marriage. It was very simple in its wording. To Julian Stormont he left a sum of five thousand pounds, to be paid out his funded property; all the rest of this property, with the sum to be realised by the sale

of the business at North Shields and its belongings—
an amount likely to be very large—was to be divided
equally between Mrs. Darrell and her stepdaughter.
Thornleigh Manor was left to Mrs. Darrell for her life,
but was to revert to Milly, or Milly's heirs, at her death;
and Milly was to be entitled to occupy her old home
until her marriage.

In the event of Milly's dying unmarried, her share of
the funded property was to be divided equally between
Mrs. Darrell and Julian Stormont, and in this case the
Thornleigh estate was to revert to Julian Stormont after the death of Mrs. Darrell. The executors to the will
were Mr. Foreman the lawyer and Mrs. Darrell.

Milly's position was now one of complete independence.
Mr. Foreman told her that after the sale of the iron-
works she would have an income of something like four
thousand a year. She had been of age for more than
six months, and there was no one to come between her
and perfect independence.

Knowing this, I felt that it was more than probable Mr.
Egerton would speedily return to renew his suit; and I
had little doubt that it would be successful. I knew how
well Milly loved him; and now that her father was gone
she could have no motive for refusing him.

'You will stay with me, won't you, Mary?' she said to
me as we sat by the fire in mournful silence that afternoon. 'You are my only comfort now, dear. I suppose I
shall remain here—for some time, at any rate. Augusta
spoke to me very graciously, and begged that I would
make this my home, according to my father's wish. We
should not interfere with each other in any way, she
said, and it was indeed more than probable she would
go on the Continent with her maid early in the spring,

and leave me sole mistress of Thornleigh. She doubted if she could ever endure the place now, she said. She is not like me, Mary. I shall always have a melancholy love for the house in which I have lived so happily with my father.'

So I remained with my dear girl, and life at Thornleigh Manor glided by in a quiet melancholy fashion. If Mrs. Darrell grieved for her dead husband, her sorrow was of a cold tearless kind; but she kept her own rooms a good deal, and we did not see much of her. The Collingwoods were full of sympathy for their 'darling Milly,' and their affection had some cheering influence upon her mind. From them she heard occasionally of Mr. Egerton, who was travelling in the wildest regions of Northern Europe. She very rarely spoke of him herself at this time; and once when I mentioned his name she checked me reproachfully.

'Don't speak about him, Mary,' she said; 'I don't want to think of him. It seems like a kind of treason against papa. It seems like taking advantage of my dear father's death.'

'Would you refuse to marry him, Milly, if he were to come back to you, now that you are your own mistress?'

'I don't know that, dear. I think I love him too much to do that. And yet it would seem like a sin against my father.'

The spring months passed, and Milly brightened a little as the days went by. She spent a deal of time amongst the poor; and I think her devotion to that duty helped her to put aside her sorrow more than anything else could have done. I was always with her, sharing in all her work; and I do not believe she had a thought hidden from me at this time.

Mrs. Darrell had not gone abroad yet. She lived a use-less, listless life, doing nothing, and caring for nothing, as it seemed. More than once she made preparations for her departure, and then changed her mind at the last moment.

Late in June we heard of Mr. Egerton's return to Cumber; and a few days after that he came to Thornleigh. Mrs. Darrell was in her own room, Milly and I alone in the drawing-room, when he called. My poor girl turned very pale, and the tears came into her eyes as she and Angus Egerton met. He spoke of her loss with extreme delicacy, and was full of tender sympathy. He had news to tell her of himself. A distant relation of his mother's had died lately, leaving him six thousand a year. He had come back to restore Cumber to its old splendour, and to take his proper place in the county.

While they were talking together in low confidential tones, not at all embarrassed by my presence, Mrs. Darrell came into the room. She was paler than usual; but there was an animation in her face that had not been there for a long time. She received Mr. Egerton very graciously, and insisted upon his staying to dinner.

The evening passed very pleasantly. I had never seen Augusta Darrell so agreeable, so fascinating, as she was that night. She touched the piano for the first time since her husband's death, and sang and played with all her old fire, keeping Angus Egerton a prisoner by the side of the piano. Hers was not music to be heard with indifference by the coldest ear.

He came again very soon, and came often. The restorations at Cumber had begun, and he insisted on our driving over to see what he was going to do. We went in compliance with this wish, and I could not but observe how anxiously he questioned Milly as to her opinion of the alterations, and how eagerly he sought for suggestions as to the arrangement and decoration of the different rooms. We spent some hours in this inspection, and stayed to luncheon, in the noble old tapestried drawing-room.

It was not very long before Mr. Egerton had renewed his suit, and had been accepted. Had Mr. Darrell lived, the altered circumstances of the suitor would, in all probability, have made some alteration in his ideas upon this subject. He could no longer have supposed Angus Egerton influenced by mercenary feelings.

My darling seemed perfectly happy in her engagement, and I shared her happiness. I was always to live with her, she said, at Cumber as well as at Thornleigh. She had told Angus this, and he was pleased that it should be so. I thought that she would have no need of me in her wedded days, and that this loving fancy of hers was not likely to be realised; but I allowed her to cherish it—time enough for our parting when it needs must come. My youth had been brightened by her love; and I should be brave enough to face the world alone when she began her new life, assured that in my day of trouble I should always find a haven in her affection.

They were to be married in the following spring. Mr. Egerton had pleaded hard for an earlier date; but Milly would not diminish her year of mourning for her father, and he was fain to submit. The appointed time was advanced from April to February. He was to take his young wife abroad, and to show her all those scenes in which his wandering life had been spent; and then they were to return to Cumber, and Milly was to begin her career as the wife of a country squire.

Julian Stormont came to Thornleigh, and heard of the engagement from Mrs. Darrell. He still occupied his old position in the business at North Shields, which had been bought by a great capitalist in the iron way. He received the news of Milly's betrothal very quietly; but he proffered her no congratulations upon the subject. I happened to be on the terrace alone with him one morning during his stay, waiting for Milly to join me, when he spoke to me about this business.

'So my cousin is going to throw herself away upon that man?' he said.

'You must not call it throwing herself away, Mr. Stormont,' I answered; 'Mr. Egerton is devoted to your cousin, and the change in his circumstances makes him a very good match for her.'

'The change in his circumstances has not changed the man,' he returned in an angry tone. 'No good can come of such a marriage.'

'You have no right to say that, Mr. Stormont.'

'I have the right given me by conviction. A happy marriage!—no, it will not be a happy marriage, be sure of that!'

He said this with a vindictive look that startled me, well as I knew that he could not feel very kindly towards Milly's lover. The words might mean little, but to me they sounded like a threat.

CHAPTER XI

Danger

The summer that year was a divine one, and we spent the greater part of our lives out of doors, driving, walking, sitting about the garden sometimes until long after dark. It was weather in which it was a kind of treason against Nature to waste an hour in the house.

We went very often for long rambles in Cumber Wood, winding up with an afternoon tea-drinking in the little study at the Priory—a home-like unceremonious entertainment which Milly delighted in. She used to seem to me on those occasions like some happy child playing at being mistress of the house.

Augusta Darrell was almost always with us. I was sorely puzzled and perplexed by her conduct at this time. It seemed to be all that a kind stepmother's could be. Her old indifferent air had quite vanished; she was more cordial, more affectionately interested in Milly's happiness than I had supposed it possible she could be. The girl was completely melted by the change in her manner, and responded to this new warmth with artless confidence in its reality.

I remembered all I had seen and all I had suspected, and I could not bring myself to believe implicitly in Milly's stepmother. There was a shadowy fear, a vague distrust in my mind, not to be put away.

As I have said, she was always with us, entering into all our simple amusements with an appearance of girlish pleasure. Our picnics, our sketching expeditions, our afternoon tea-parties at the Priory, our croquet-matches with the Rector's daughters, seemed all alike agreeable to her. I noticed that her toilet was always perfect on theses occasions, and that she neglected no art which could add to her attractiveness; but she never in any way attempted to absorb Mr. Egerton's attention—she never ignored his position as Milly's accepted suitor.

For a long time I was deceived by her manner—almost convinced that if she had ever cared for Angus Egerton in the past, it was a passion that had died out of her heart. But there came a day when one look of hers betrayed the real state of the case, and showed me that all this newly-awakened regard for Milly, and pleasant participation in her happiness, had been only a careful piece of acting. It was nothing but a look—one earnest, despairing, passionate look—that told me this, but it was a look that betrayed the secret of a life. From that moment I never again trusted Augusta Darrell.

With the beginning of autumn the weather changed, and there came a dull rainy season. Trouble came to us with the change of the weather. There was a good deal of low fever about Thornleigh, and Milly caught it. She had never neglected her visit amongst the poor, even in favour of those pleasant engagements with Angus Egerton; and there is no doubt she had taken the fever from some of the cottagers.

She was not alarmingly ill, nor was the fever supposed to be contagious, except under certain conditions. Mr. Hale, the Thornleigh doctor, made very light of the business, and assured us that his patient would be as well as ever in a week's time. But in the mean while my dear girl kept her room, and I nursed her, with the assistance of her devoted little maid.

Mr. Egerton came every day, generally twice a day, to inquire about the invalid's progress, and would stay for half an hour, or longer, talking to Mrs. Darrell or to me. He was very much depressed by this illness, and impatient for his betrothed's recovery. He had been strictly forbidden to see her, as perfect repose was an essential condition to her well-being.

The week was nearly over, and Milly had improved considerably. She was now able to sit up for an hour or two every day, and the doctor promised Mr. Egerton that she should be in the drawing-room early in the following week. The weather had been incessantly wet during this time—dull, hopeless, perpetual rain day after day, without a break in the leaden sky. But at last there came a fine evening, and I went down to the terrace to take a solitary walk after my long imprisonment. It was between six and seven o'clock; Milly was asleep, and there was no probability of my being wanted in the sick-room for half an hour or so. I left ample instructions with my handy little assistant, and went down for my constitutional, muffled in a warm shawl.

It was dusk when I went out, and everything was unusually quiet, not a leaf was stirring in the stagnant atmosphere. Late as it was, the evening was almost oppressively warm, and I was glad to throw off my shawl. I walked up and down the terrace in front of the Hall for about ten minutes, and then went round towards the drawing-room windows. Before I had quite reached the first of these, I was arrested by a sound so strange that I stopped involuntarily to listen. Throughout all that followed, I had no time to consider whether I was doing right or wrong in hearing what I did hear; but I believe if I had had ample leisure for deliberation, it would have come to the same thing—I should have listened. What I heard was of such vital consequence to the girl I loved, that I think loyalty to her outweighed any treachery against the speaker.

The strange sound that brought me to a standstill close to the wide-open window was the sound of a woman's passionate sobbing—such a storm of weeping as one does not hear many times in a life. I have never heard anything like it until that night.

Angus Egerton's sonorous voice broke in upon those tempestuous sobs almost angrily:

'Augusta, this is supreme folly.'

The sobs went on for some minutes longer unchecked. I heard his step sounding heavily as he walked up and down the room.

'I am waiting to hear the meaning of all this,' he said by and by. 'I suppose there is some meaning.'

'O Angus, is it so easy for you to forget the past?'

'It was forgotten long ago,' he answered, 'by both of us, I should think. When my mother bribed you to leave Ilfracombe, you bartered my love and my happiness for the petty price she was able to pay. I was a weak fool in those days, and I took the business to heart bitterly enough, God knows; but the lesson was a useful one, and it served its turn. I have never trusted myself to love any woman since that day, till I met the pure young creature who is to be my wife. Her truth is above all doubt; she will not sell her birthright for a mess of pottage.'

'The mess of pottage was not for me, Angus. It was my father's bargain, not mine. I was told that you had done with me—that you had never meant to marry me. Yes, Angus, your mother told me that with her own lips—told me that she interfered to save me from misery and dishonour. And then I was hurried off to a cheap French convent, to learn to provide for myself. A couple of years' schooling was the price I received for my broken heart. That was what your mother called making me a lady. I think I should have gone mad in those two dreary years, if it had not been for my passionate love of music. I gave myself up to that with my whole soul; my heart was dead; and they told me I made more progress in two years than other girls made in six. I had nothing else to live for.'

'Except the hope of a rich husband,' said Mr. Egerton, with a sneer.

'O God, how cruel a man can to be a woman he has once loved!' cried Mrs. Darrell passionately. 'Yes, I did marry a rich man, Angus; but I never schemed or tried to win him. The chance came to me without a hope or a thought of mine. It was the chance of rescue from the dreariest life of drudgery that a poor dependent creature ever lived, and I took it. But I have never forgotten you, Angus Egerton, not for one hour of my life.'

'I am sorry you should have taken the trouble to remember me,' he answered very coldly. 'For some years of my life I made it my chief business to forget you, and all the pain connected with our acquaintance; and having succeeded in doing that, it seems a pity that we should disturb the stagnant waters of that dead lake which men call the past.'

'Would to God that we had never met again!' she said.

'I can quite echo that aspiration, if we are likely to have many such scenes as this.'

'Cruel—cruel!' she muttered. 'O Angus, I have been so patient! I have clung to hope in the face of despair. When my husband died I fancied your old love would reawaken. How can such things die? I thought it was to me you would come back—to me, whom you once loved so passionately—not to that girl. You came back to her, and still I was patient. I set myself against her, to win back your love. Yes, Angus, I hoped to do that till very lately. And then I began to see that it was all useless. She is younger and handsomer than I.'

'She is better than you, Augusta. It was not her beauty that won me, but something nobler and rarer than beauty: it was her perfect nature. The more faulty we are ourselves, the more fondly we cling to a good woman. But I don't want to say hard things, Augusta. Pray let us put all this folly aside at once and for ever. You took your course in the past, and it has landed you in a very prosperous position. Let me take mine in the present, and let us be friends, if possible.'

'You know that it is not possible. We must be all the world to each other, or the bitterest enemies.'

'I shall never be your enemy, Mrs. Darrell.'

'But I am yours; yes, I am yours from this night, and hers. You think I can look on tamely, and see you devoted to that girl! I have only been playing a part. I thought it was in my power to win you back.'

All this was said with a kind of passionate reckless-
ness, as if the speaker, having suddenly thrown off her
mask, scarcely cared how utterly she degraded herself.

'Good-night, Mrs. Darrell. You will think of these
things more wisely to-morrow. Let us be civil to each
other, at least, while circumstances bring us together;
and for God's sake be kind to your stepdaughter! Do
not think of her as a rival; my love for you had died long
before I saw her. You need bear no malice against her
on that account. Good-night.'

'Good-night.'

I heard the drawing-room door open and shut, and
knew that he was gone. I walked on past the open windows, not caring if Mrs. Darrell saw me. It might be
better for Milly, perhaps, that she should know I had
heard her secret, and had been put upon my guard. But
I do not think she saw me.

It was about a quarter of an hour later when I went in,
and it was quite dark by that time. In the hall I met
Mrs. Darrell, dressed for walking.

'I am going round the shrubberies, Miss Crofton,' she
said. 'Insupportably close to-night, is it not? I think we
shall all have the fever if this weather lasts.'

She did not wait for my answer, but passed out quickly.
I went back to Milly's room, and found her still sleeping peacefully. Ten minutes afterwards I heard the rain
beating against the windows, and knew that it had set
in for a wet night.

'Mrs. Darrell will not be able to go far,' I thought.

I sat by the bedside for some time thinking of what I
had heard. It was something to have had so strong a

proof of Angus Egerton's loyalty to my dear girl; and assured of that, I did not fear Mrs. Darrell's malice. Yet I could not help wishing that the marriage had been appointed for an earlier date, and that the time which stepmother and daughter were to spend together had been shorter.

Milly woke, and sat up for about half an hour, supported by pillows, to take a cup of tea, while I talked to her a little about the pleasantest subjects I could think of. She asked if Mr. Egerton had been at Thornleigh that evening.

'Yes, dear, he has been.'

'Did you see him, Mary?'

'No; I did not see him.'

She gave a little disappointed sigh. It was her delight to hear me repeat his messages to her, word for word, ever so many times over.

'Then you have nothing to tell me about him, dear?'

'Nothing; except that I know he loves you.'

'Ah, Mary, there was a time when you doubted him.'

'That time is quite past and gone, dear.'

She kissed me as she gave me back her cup and saucer, and promised to go to sleep again, while I went to my room to write a long letter home.

I was occupied in this way for more than an hour; and then, having sealed my letter, went down with it to the hall, to put it on a table where all letters intended to be taken to the post in the morning were placed over-night.

It was nearly ten o'clock by this time, and I was startled by the sound of the hall-door opening softly from without, while I was putting down my letter. I looked round quietly, and saw Mrs. Darrell coming in, with dripping garments.

'Good gracious me!' I cried involuntarily; 'have you been out all this time in the rain, Mrs. Darrell?'

'Yes, I have been out in the rain, Miss Crofton,' she answered in a vexed impatient tone. 'Is that so very shocking to your sober ideas of propriety? I could not endure the house to-night. One has feverish fancies sometimes—at least I have; and I preferred being out in the rain to not being out at all. Good-night.'

She gave me a haughty nod, and ran up-stairs with a quick light step. The old butler came to lock and bolt the hall-door as the clock struck ten, according to unalterable custom; and I went back to my room, wondering what could have kept Mrs. Darrell out so long— whether she had been upon some special errand, or had only been wandering about the grounds in a purposeless way.

For some days Milly went on very well; then there came a little change for the worse. The symptoms were not quite so favourable. Mr. Hale assured us that there was no reason for alarm, the recovery was only a little retarded. He had not the least doubt that all would go well. Mr. Egerton was very quick to take fright, however, and insisted on Dr. Lomond, a famous provincial physician, being summoned immediately from Manchester.

The great man came, and his opinion coincided entirely with that of Mr. Hale. There was not the slightest cause for fear. Careful nursing and quiet were the two essential points. The patient's mind was to be made as happy as possible. The physician made minute inquiries as to the arrangements for attendance in the sick-room, and suggested a professional nurse. But I pleaded so hard against this, assuring him of my capacity for doing much more than I had to do, that he gave way, and consented to Milly being waited only by myself and her maid.

Mrs. Darrell was present during this conversation, and I was rather surprised by her taking my side of the question with regard to the nursing, as it was her usual habit to oppose me upon all subjects. To-day she was singularly gracious.

Another week went by, and there was no change for the better, nor any very perceptible change for the worse. The patient was a little weaker, and suffered from a depression of mind, against which all my efforts were vain.

Angus Egerton came twice daily during this week, but he rarely saw Mrs. Darrell. I think he studiously avoided meeting her after that painful scene in the drawing-room. It was for me he inquired, and he used to come up-stairs to the corridor outside Milly's room, and stand there talking to me in a low voice, and feeling a kind of satisfaction, I believe, in being so near his darling.

Once I ventured to tell her that he was there, and to let him speak a few words for her to hear. But the sound of the voice she loved so well had such an agitating effect upon her, that I sorely repented my imprudence, and took good care not to repeat it.

So the days went by, in that slow dreary way in which time passes when those we love are ill; and it seemed, in the dead calm of the sick-room, as if all the business of life had come to a stand-still.

I did not see much of Mrs. Darrell during this period. She came to Milly's door two or three times a day to ask about her progress, with all appearance of affection and anxiety; but throughout the rest of the day she remained secluded in her own rooms. I noticed that she had a wan haggard look at this time, like that of a person who had existed for a long while without sleep; but this in no manner surprised me, after that scene in the drawing-room.

As the time went by, I felt that my strength was beginning to fail, and I sadly feared that we might have at last to employ the professional aid which the Manchester physician had suggested. I had slept very little from the beginning of Milly's illness, being too anxious to sleep when I had the opportunity of doing so; and I now began to suffer from the effects of this prolonged sleeplessness. But I struggled resolutely against fatigue, determined to see my dear girl through the fever if possible; and I succeeded wonderfully, by the aid of unlimited cups of strong tea, and always ably seconded by Susan Dodd, Milly's devoted maid.

Between us we two performed all the duties of the sick-room. The medicines, wine, soups, jellies, and all things required for the invalid were kept in the dressing-room, which communicated with the bedroom by one door, and had another door opening on to the corridor.

The sick-room, which was very large and airy, was by this means kept free from all litter; and Susan and I took pleasure in making it look bright and fresh. I used to fetch a bouquet from the garden every morning for the little table by the bed. At the very commencement of Milly's illness I had missed Peter, Mrs. Thatcher's grandson. I asked one of the men what had become of him, and was told that he had taken the fever and was lying ill at his grandmother's cottage. I mentioned this to Mrs. Darrell, and asked her permission to send him some wine and other little comforts, to which she assented.

The Manchester physician came a second time after a week's interval, and on this occasion he was not so positive in his opinion as to the case. He did not consider that there was peril as yet, he said; but the patient was weaker, and he was by no means satisfied. He prescribed a change of medicine, repeated his injunctions about care and quiet; and so departed, after requesting Mr. Hale to telegraph for him in the event of any change for the worse.

I was a good deal depressed by his manner this time, and went back to my dear girl's room with a heavier heart than I had known since her illness began.

It was my habit to take whatever sleep I could in the course of the afternoon, leaving Susan Dodd on guard, so as to be able to sit up all night. Susan had begged very hard to share this night-watching, but I insisted upon her taking her usual rest, so as to be bright and fresh in the day. I felt the night-work was the more important duty, and could trust that to no one but myself.

Unfortunately it happened very often that I was quite unable to sleep when I went to my room in the afternoon to lie down. Half my time I used to lie there wide awake thinking of my darling girl, and praying for her speedy recovery. On the afternoon that followed the Manchester doctor's second visit I went to my room as usual; but I was more than ever disinclined to sleep. For the first time since the fever began I felt a horrible dread that the end might be fatal; and I lay tossing restlessly from side to side, meditating on every word and look of the physician's, and trying to convince myself that there was no real ground for my alarm.

I had been lying awake like this for more than an hour, when I heard the door of Milly's dressing-room—which was close to my door—closed softly; and with a nervous quickness to take alarm I sprang up, and went out into the corridor, thinking that Susan was coming to summon me. I found myself face to face, not with Susan Dodd, but with Mrs. Darrell.

She gave a little start at seeing me, and stood with her hand still upon the handle of the dressing-room door, looking at me with the strangest expression I ever saw in any human countenance. Alarm, defiance, hatred—what was it?

'I thought you were asleep,' she said.

'I have not been able to sleep this afternoon.'

'You are a bad person for a nurse, Miss Crofton, if you cannot sleep at will. I am afraid you are nervous, too, by the way you darted out of the room just now.'

'I heard that door shut, and thought Susan was coming to call me.'

'I had just been in to see how the invalid was going on—that is all.'

She passed me, and went back to her own apartments, which were on the other side of the house. I felt that it was quite useless trying to sleep; so I returned to my room only to change my dressing-gown for my dress, and then went back to Milly. She had been sleeping very quietly, Susan told me.

'I suppose you told Mrs. Darrell that all was going on well when she came to inquire just now?' I said.

'Mrs. Darrell hasn't been since you went to lie down, miss,' the girl answered, looking surprised at my question.

'Why, Susan, you must surely forget. Mrs. Darrell was in the dressing-room scarcely ten minutes ago. I heard her coming out, and went to see who was there. Didn't she come in here to inquire about Miss Darrell?'

'No, indeed, miss.'

'Then I suppose she must have peeped in at the door and seen that Miss Darrell was asleep,' I said.

'I don't see how she could have opened that door without my hearing her, miss. It was shut fast, I know.'

It had been shut when I went in through the dressing-room. I was puzzled by this incident, small as it was. I knew that Augusta Darrell hated her stepdaughter, and I could not bear to think of that secret enemy hovering about the sick-room. I was puzzled too by the look which I had seen in her face—no common look, and not easy to be understood. That she hated me, I had no doubt; but there had been fear as well as aversion in that look, and I could not imagine any possible reason for her fearing such an insignificant person as myself.

The rest of that evening and night passed without any event worth recording. I kept the door of communication between the bedroom and dressing-room wide open all night, determined that Augusta Darrell should not be in that room without my knowledge; but the night passed, and she never came near us.

When I went into the garden early the next morning to gather the flowers for Milly's room, I found Peter at work again. He looked very white and feeble, scarcely fit to be about just yet; but there he was, sweeping the fallen leaves into little heaps, ready for his barrow. He came to me while I was cutting the late roses for my bouquet, and asked after Milly. When I had answered him he loitered by me for a little in a curious way, as if he wanted to say something else; but I was too full of my own thoughts and cares to pay much attention to him.

The next day, and the next, brought no change in my darling, and I was growing every hour more anxious. I could see that Mr. Hale was puzzled and uneasy, though he said he saw no reason for telegraphing to Manchester, yet awhile. He was very attentive, and was reputed to be very clever; and I knew that he was really attached to Milly, whom he had attended from her infancy.

Angus Egerton saw me twice every day; and these brief interviews had now become very painful to me. I found it so difficult to cheer him with hopeful words, when my own heart was hourly growing heavier, and the fears that had been vague and shadowy were gathering strength and shape. I was very tired, but I held out resolutely; and I had never once slept for so much as a quarter of an hour upon my watch, until the second night after that meeting with Mrs. Darrell at the door of the dressing-room.

That night I was seized with an unconquerable sleepiness, about an hour after I had dismissed Susan Dodd. The room was very quiet, not a sound except the ticking of the pretty little clock upon the mantelpiece. Milly was fast asleep, and I was sitting on a low chair by the fire trying to read, when my drowsiness overcame me, my heavy eyelids fell, and I went off into a feverish kind of slumber, in which I was troubled with an uneasy consciousness that I ought to be awake.

I had slept in this way for a little more than an hour, when I suddenly started up broad awake. [In] the intense quiet of the room I had heard a sound like the chinking of glass, and I fancied that Milly had stirred.

There was a table near her bed, with a glass of cooling drink and a bottle of water upon it. I thought she must have stretched out her hand for this glass, and that in so doing she had pushed the glass against the bottle; but to my surprise I found her lying quite still, and fast asleep. The sound must have come from some other direction—from the dressing-room, perhaps.

I went into the dressing-room. There was no one there. No trace of the smallest disturbance among the things. The medicine-bottles and the medicine-glass stood on the little table exactly as I had left them. I was very careful and precise in my arrangement of these things, and it would have been difficult for the slightest interference with them to have escaped me. What could that sound have been—some accidental shiver of the glass, stirred by a breath of wind, one of those mysterious movements of inanimate objects which are so apt to occur in the dead hours of the night, and which seem always more or less ghostly to a nervous watcher? Could it have been only accidental? or had Mrs. Darrell been prowling stealthily in and out of that room again?

Why should she have been there? What could her secret coming and going mean? What purpose could she have in hovering about the sick girl? what could her hatred profit itself by such uneasy watchfulness, unless— Unless what? An icy coldness came over me, and I shook like a leaf, as a dreadful thought took shape in my mind. What if that desperate woman's hatred took the most awful form? what if her secret presence in that room meant murder?

I took up the medicine-bottle and examined it minutely. In colour, in odour, in taste, the medicine seemed to me exactly what it had been from the time it had been altered, in accordance with the Manchester doctor's second prescription. Mr. Hale's label was on the bottle, and the quantity of the contents was exactly what it had been after I gave Milly her last dose—one dose gone out of the full bottle.

'O, no, no, no,' I thought to myself; 'I must be mad to imagine anything so awful. A woman may be weak, and wicked, and jealous, when she has loved as intensely as this woman seems to have loved Angus Egerton; but that is no reason she should become a murderess.'

I stood with the medicine-bottle in my hand sorely perplexed. What could I do? Should I suspend the medicine for to-night, at the risk of retarding the cure? or should I give it in spite of that half suspicion that it had been tampered with?

What ground had I for such a suspicion? At that moment nothing but the sound that had awakened me, the chinking sound of one glass knocked against another.

Had I really heard any such sound, or had it only been a delusion of my half sleeping brain? While I stood weighing this question, a sudden recollection flashed across my mind, and I had no longer ground for doubt.

The cork of the medicine-bottle, when I gave Milly her last dose, had been too large for the bottle; so much so, that I had found it difficult to put it in again after giving the medicine. The cork of the bottle which I now held in my hand went in loosely enough. It was a smaller and an older-looking cork. This decided me. I placed the bottle under lock and key in Milly's wardrobe, and I gave her no more medicine that night.

There was no fear of my sleeping at my post after this. My thoughts for the rest of that night were full of horror and bewilderment. My course seemed clear enough, in one respect. The proper person to confide in would be Mr. Hale. He would be able to discover whether the medicine had been tampered with, and it would be his business to protect his patient.

CHAPTER XII

Defeated

I went down to the garden for the flowers as usual next morning, as I did not wish to make any palpable change in my arrangements; but before leaving the room I impressed upon Susan Dodd the necessity of remaining with her mistress during every moment of my absence, though I knew I had little need to counsel carefulness. Nothing was more unlikely than that Susan would neglect her duty for a moment.

Peter came again, as he had come to me on the previous morning. Again he lingered about me, as if he had something more to say, and could not take courage to say it. This time the strangeness of his manner aroused my curiosity, and I asked him if he had anything particular to say to me.

'You must be quick, Peter, whatever it is,' I said; 'for I am in a great hurry to get back to Miss Darrell.'

'There is something I want to say, miss,' he answered, twisting his ragged straw hat round and round in his bony hands, in a nervous way,—'something I should like to say, but I'm naught but a poor fondy, and don't know how to begin. Only you've been very good to Peter, you see, miss, sending wine and such things when I was ill, and I ain't afeard o' you, as I am o' some folks.'

'The wine was not mine, Peter. Be quick, please; tell me what you want to say.'

'I can't come to it very easy, miss. It's something awful-like to tell on.'

'Something awful?'

The boy had looked round him with a cautious glance, and was now standing close to me, with his light blue eyes fixed upon my face in a very earnest way.

'Speak out, Peter,' I said; 'you needn't be afraid of me.'

'It happened when I was ill, you see, miss, and I've sometimes thought as it might be no more than a dream. I had a many dreams while I were lying on that little bed in grandmother's room, wicked dreams, and this might be one of them; and yet it's real-like, and there isn't the muddle in it that there is in the other dreams.'

'What is it, Peter? O, pray, pray be quick!'

'I'm a-coming to it, miss. Is it wicked for folks to kill theirselves?'

'Is it wicked? Of course it is—desperately wicked; a sin that can never be repented of.'

'Then I know one that's going to do it.'

'Who?'

'Mrs. Darrell.'

He gave a solemn nod, and stood staring at me with wide-open awe-stricken eyes.

'How do you know that?'

'It was one dark night, when it was raining hard—I could hear it drip, drip, drip upon the roof just over where I was lying. It was when I was very bad, and lay still all day and couldn't speak. But I knew what grandmother said to me, and I knew everything that was going on, though I didn't seem to—that was the curious part of it. I had been asleep for a bit, and I woke up all of a sudden, and heard some one talking to grandmother in the next room—the door wasn't wide open, only ajar. I shouldn't have known who it was, for I'm not quick at telling voices, like other folks; but I heard grandmother call her Mrs. Darrell; and I heard the lady say that when one was sick and tired of life, and had no one left to live for, it was best to die; and grandmother laughed, and says yes, there wasn't much to live for, leastways not for such as her. And then they talked a little more; and then by and by Mrs. Darrell asked her for some stuff—I didn't hear the name of it, for Mrs. Darrell only whispered it. Grandmother says no, and stuck to it for a good time; but Mrs. Darrell offered her money, and then more and more money. She says it couldn't matter whether she got the stuff from her or from any one else. She could get it easily enough, she says, in any large town. And she didn't know as she should use it, she says. It was more likely than not she never would; but she wanted to have it by her, so as to feel she was able to put an end to her life, if ever it grew burdensome to her. "You'll never use it against any one else?" says grandmother; and Mrs. Darrell says who was there she could use it against, and what harm need she wish to anybody; she was rich enough, and had nothing to gain from anybody's death. So at last, after a deal of talk,

grandmother gave her the stuff; and I heard her count-
ing out money—I think it was a hundred pounds—and
then she went away in the rain.'

I remembered that night upon which Mrs. Darrell had
stayed out so long in the rain—the night that followed
her stormy interview with Angus Egerton.

I told Peter that he had done quite right in telling me
this, and begged him not to mention it to any one else
until I gave him permission to do so. I went back to
Milly's room directly afterwards, and waited there for
Mr. Hale's coming.

While I was taking my breakfast, Mrs. Darrell came to
make her usual inquiries. I ran into the dressing-room
to meet her. While she was questioning me about the
invalid, I saw her look at the table where the medicine
had always been until that morning, and I knew that
she missed the bottle.

After she had made her inquiries, she stood for a few
moments hesitating, and then said abruptly,

'I should like to see Mr. Hale when he comes this morning. I want to hear what he says about his patient. He
will be here almost immediately, I suppose; so I will
stay in Milly's room till he comes.'

She went into the bedroom, bent over the invalid for a
few minutes, talking in a gentle sympathetic voice, and
then took her place by the bedside. It was evident to me
that she had suspected something from the removal of
the medicine, and that she intended to prevent my seeing Mr. Hale alone.

'You took your medicine regularly last night, I suppose, Milly?' she inquired presently, when I had seated

myself at a little table by the window and was sipping my tea.

'I don't think you gave me quite so many doses last night, did you, Mary?' said the invalid, in her feeble voice. 'I fancy you were more merciful than usual.'

'It was very wrong of Miss Crofton to neglect your medicine. Mr. Hale will be extremely angry when he hears of it.'

'I do not think Milly will be much worse for the omission,' I answered quietly.

After this we sat silently waiting for the doctor's appearance. He came in about a quarter of an hour, and pronounced himself better pleased with his patient than he had been the night before. There had been a modification of the more troublesome symptoms of the fever towards morning.

I told him of my omission to give the medicine.

'That was very wrong,' he said.

'Yet you see she had a better night, Mr. Hale. I suppose that medicine was intended to modify those attacks of sickness from which she has suffered so much?'

'To prevent them altogether, if possible.'

'That is very strange. It really appears to me that the medicine always increases the tendency to sickness.'

Mr. Hale shook his head impatiently.

'You don't know what you are talking about, Miss Crofton,' he said.

'May I say a few words to you alone, if you please?'

Mrs. Darrell rose, with a hurried anxious look.

'What can you have to say to Mr. Hale alone, Miss Crofton?' she asked.

'It is about herself, perhaps,' said the doctor kindly. 'I have told her all along that she would be knocked up by this nursing; and now I daresay she begins to find I am right.'

'Yes,' I said, 'it is about myself I want to speak.'

Mrs. Darrell went to one of the windows, and stood with her face turned away from us, looking out. I followed Mr. Hale into the dressing-room.

I unlocked the wardrobe, took out the medicine-bottle, and told the doctor my suspicions of the previous night. He listened to me with grave attention, but with an utterly incredulous look.

'A nervous fancy of yours, no doubt, Miss Crofton,' he said; 'however, I'll take the medicine back to my surgery and analyse it.'

'I have something more to tell you, Mr. Hale.'

'Indeed!'

I repeated, word for word, what Peter had told me about Mrs. Darrell's visit to his grandmother.

'It is a very extraordinary business,' he said; 'but I cannot imagine that Mrs. Darrell would be capable of such a hideous crime. What motive could she have for such an act?'

'I do not feel justified in speaking quite plainly upon that subject, Mr. Hale; but I have reason to know that Mrs. Darrell has a very bitter feeling about her stepdaughter.'

'I cannot think the thing you suspect possible. However, the medicine shall be analysed; and we will take all precautions for the future. I will send you another bottle immediately, in a sealed packet. You will take notice that the seal is unbroken before you use the medicine.'

He showed me his crest on a seal at the end of his pencil-case, and then departed. The medicine came a quarter of an hour later in a sealed packet. This time I brought the bottle into the sick-room, and placed it on the mantelpiece, where it was impossible for any one to touch it.

When Mr. Hale came for his second visit, there was a grave and anxious look in his face. He was very well satisfied with the appearance of the patient, however, and pronounced that there was a change for the better—slight, of course, but quite as much as could be expected in so short a time. He beckoned me out of the room, and I went down-stairs with him, leaving Susan Dodd with Milly.

'I am going to speak to Mrs. Darrell, and you had better come with me,' he said.

She was in the library. Mr. Hale went in, and I followed him. She was sitting at the table, with writing materials scattered before her; but she was not writing. She had a strange preoccupied air; but at the sight of Mr. Hale she rose suddenly, and looked at him with a deadly white face.

'Is she worse?' she asked.

'No, Mrs. Darrell; she is better,' he answered sternly. 'I find that we have been the dupes of some secret enemy of this dear child's. There has been an attempt at murder going on under our very eyes. Poison has been mixed with the medicine sent by me—a slow poison.

Happily for us the poisoner has been a little too cautious for the success of the crime. The doses administered have been small enough to leave the chance of recovery. An accident awakened Miss Crofton's suspicions last night, and she very wisely discontinued the medicine. I have analysed it since she gave it me, and find that a certain portion of irritant poison has been mixed with it.'

For some moments after he had finished speaking Mrs. Darrell remained silent, looking at him fixedly with that awful death-like face.

'Who can have done such a thing?' she asked at last, in a half-mechanical way.

'You must be a better judge of that question than I,' answered Mr. Hale. 'Is there any one in this house inimical to your stepdaughter?'

'No one, that I know of.'

'We have two duties before us, Mrs. Darrell: the first, to protect our patient from the possibility of any farther attempt of this kind; the second, to trace the hand that has done this work. I shall telegraph to Leeds immediately for a professional nurse, to relieve Miss Crofton in the care of the sick-room; and I shall communicate at once with the police, in order that this house may be placed under surveillance.'

Mrs. Darrell said not a word, either in objection or assent, to this. She seated herself by the table again, and began trifling idly with the writing materials before her.

'You will do what is best, of course, Mr. Hale,' she said, after a long pause; 'you are quite at liberty to act in this matter according to your own discretion.'

'Thanks; it is a matter in which my responsibility entitles me to a certain amount of power. I shall telegraph to Dr. Lomond, asking him to come down to-morrow. Whatever doubt you may entertain of my judgment will be dispelled when I am supported by his opinion.'

'Of course; but I have not expressed any doubt of your judgment.'

We left her immediately after this—left her sitting before the table, with her restless hands turning over the papers.

The servant who went in search of her at seven o'clock that evening, when dinner was served, found her sitting there still, with a sealed letter lying on the table before her; but her head had fallen across the cushioned arm of the chair—she had been dead some hours.

There was a post-mortem examination and an inquest. Mrs. Darrell had taken poison. The jury brought in a verdict of suicide while in a state of unsound mind. The act seemed too causeless for sanity. Her strange absent ways had attracted the attention of the servants for some time past, and the evidence of her own maid respecting her restlessness and irritability for the last few months influenced the minds of coroner and jury.

The letter found lying on the table before her was addressed to Angus Egerton. He declined to communicate its contents when questioned about it at the inquest. Milly progressed towards recovery slowly but surely from the hour in which I stopped the suspected medicine. The time came when we were obliged to tell her of her stepmother's awful death; but she never knew the attempt that had been made on her own life, or the atmosphere of hatred in which she had lived.

We left Thornleigh for Scarborough as soon as she was well enough to be moved, and only returned in the early spring, in time for my darling's wedding.

She has now been married nearly seven years, during which time her life has been very bright and happy—a life of almost uncheckered sunshine. She has carried out her idea of our friendship to the very letter; and we have never been separated, except during her honeymoon and my own visits home. Happily for my sense of independence, there are now plenty of duties for me to perform at Cumber Priory, where I am governess to a brood of pretty children, who call me auntie, and hold me scarcely second to their mother in their warm young hearts. Angus Egerton is a model country squire and master of the hounds; and he and his wife enjoy an unbroken popularity among rich and poor. Peter is under-gardener at the Priory, and no longer lives with his grandmother, who left her cottage soon after Mrs. Darrell's suicide, and is supposed to have gone to London.